CW00407076

Punching
Professor Pargus

David Ward

Copyright © 2016 David Ward

pargusbooks@gmail.com

Kenneth's office was a mess. He was by no means fastidious, but this was a step too far. All of the drawers had been pulled out of his desk, there were books and papers scattered on the floor. A bottle of whisky appeared to have been hurled against the wall.

I noted he hadn't welcomed me in his usual forthright manner. His general bearing seemed off. He was slumped at his desk at a peculiar angle. I waved at him and then broke into a light jig to try and attract his attention. No response. I don't know why, but there was just something about the whole scene that didn't sit right with me.

I approached the desk gingerly, as one might a tiger or similar jungle cat. A light prod on Kenneth's head seemed appropriate. Still nothing. I prodded again, harder this time, really putting my finger into it. Then I noticed that there was a large knife sticking out of his back. Hmm. I knew Kenneth, and could say with some degree of certainty he would not enjoy a large knife sticking out of his back. Strange then, that he was just lying there.

Some moments passed. Slowly at first and then all of a sudden the realisation hit me. The smoke cleared to reveal the cold hard facts. How could I have been so stupid? Kenneth must not have realised there was a large knife sticking out of his back.

This placed me in a tricky situation; if he wasn't going to respond, how was I to convey the severity of the situation?

I like to think I've led a full life. But I had never pulled a large knife from the back of a close friend before. Maybe I should have taken that gap year after all. To be honest though, there didn't seem much to it. Being well versed in the story of King Arthur and the sword in the stone, I imagined it to be of a similar principle.

'I'm going to pull the large knife out of your back,' I told Kenneth.

I stood behind him, took a firm grip of the handle and a deep breath. I steeled myself. Seconds passed. It was now or never. Now. Or never. I had to pull the large knife out of Kenneth's back now or never. Still, time ticked by. This was now or never stuff.

Just as I was ruminating on the etymology of the word 'never' the office door opened. It was Cara, Kenneth's secretary.

'Oh my God!' she screamed. 'I'm calling the police!' She ran out of the office. This seemed a little extreme. I was going to pull the knife out eventually; there was no need to get the police involved. Was this even the kind of thing they dealt with? Surely it was more of a job for the fire brigade, or maybe an unskilled labourer? Still, there was nothing much to be done about it. The police were on their way. I relaxed my grip on the handle and took my customary seat opposite Kenneth.

When they eventually arrived, I was astonished by the amount of personnel they had brought to a routine large-knife-in-back call out. Fully six officers burst into the office, three of them immediately seeing fit to drag me from my chair and pin me against the wall.

It was hard not to be offended. You don't reposition a harmless chair dweller wall-wards without a solid reason. And why *were* there so many of them here? Surely removing a knife from a back was a one person job, (two at a push, if they needed someone to hold the shoulders)? This is where our taxes go.

I had to get to the bottom of this. There was far too much noise and commotion and general flailing around. My right arm was beginning to lose feeling. Answers were needed as to why they were holding me so tightly, why there were so many of them, as well as what they planned to do to help out Kenneth. I had to be incisive and sharp, burrow under the ground to get to the root of the problem so that a beautiful flowery solution could grow.

I looked at each of the three men holding me and addressed the one with the smallest head. 'What's all this about?' I said.

*

Around the eighth hour of sitting in the police cell I began to feel a little bored. It was clear that someone, somewhere, at some stage had got the wrong idea about something. Replaying the events of the day it was hard to see when this could have happened.

Arguably it could have been when I stamped on the small headed policeman's foot, using the confusion this caused to free my arms and evade the officers with an admirable fleetness of foot. If I wasn't going to get a straight answer then the situation called for decisive action. Nimbly, I then made my way over to Kenneth and grabbed hold of the knife. With an almighty pull, I removed it from its fleshing dwelling.

'See how easy that was!' I had shouted at the police officers whilst waving the bloody knife at them.

Their reaction was not what I had anticipated. Rather than congratulating me on my moment of glory they appeared perturbed, scared even. That they could have grasped the wrong end of the stick to such a degree struck me as hilarious. I started to giggle. And well, I've always been the sort for whom a trickle of a giggle invariably transforms into a cataract of hysteria. Soon I was bent double over the desk much like Kenneth. In the midst of my laughter, I banged my fist down on the table in mirth, forgetting that I was holding the knife. It skittered out of my hand and the policemen were on me like a pack of hyenas or similar jungle cat. In no time at all, I was being carted out of the building with nary a 'well done' or 'good job with the knife pulling' from any of them.

So there, I sat in the cell, bored and wishing I had thought to bring a magazine. But if, as it seemed, I was to be in there for a while, I thought I might as well get some exercise. I managed only three press ups and sit ups before collapsing in exhaustion. Perhaps it wasn't the best idea to attempt them simultaneously. This segued into a well-earned snooze and I was awoken only by the cell door screeching open.

I was led into another, smaller room with a table in the middle and mirror covering each wall. 'No room for press ups in here, eh?' I bantered with the police officer who had escorted me. He didn't reply. None of the policemen I had spoken too had any great level of chat. An odd bunch.

The silent policeman departed. After twenty minutes alone made entertaining only by the interesting noises I discovered I could make if I hummed whilst tapping on my Adam's apple, the door opened. The man who entered didn't look like any look like the other policemen. For one thing, he wasn't wearing a uniform. Not a policeman's uniform anyway. For all I knew an ill-fitting grey suit could be de rigueur for any number of occupations. I made a mental note to ask him at some stage what he did for a living.

Though undeniably a tall gentleman, he had a certain sadness in his eyes which made me wonder if he realised how tall he was. I estimated him to be around forty years old and Caucasian. Aside from that he was a complete mystery man.

He took a seat opposite me. 'Hello, Cudgel. My name is Detective-...'

'Mystery Man!' I said.

'What?' he replied.

'What?' I countered

'What do you mean, "*Mystery Man*"?'

'What do you *mean*, Mystery Man?'

Mystery Man sighed and took off his glasses (he was wearing glasses! How did I miss that?). Then he sighed again, a deeper sigh this time, a sigh that seemed to conjure all of the despair and malaise this world has to offer and expel it through two badly shaven cheeks.

'Are you joking?' he said.

I frowned and composed myself. I drew myself up straight in my chair and folded my hands neatly on the table.

'Are *you* joking?' I said.

Somewhat surprisingly, Mystery Man chose this moment to slap me hard on the side of the head. I am no stranger to physical violence amongst friends but felt Mystery Man should have had the good grace to preface it with some sort of warning. Kenneth, in the pre-knife-in-back-era would always give a verbal introduction, something along the lines of, 'If you don't leave right now I'm going to punch you in the face.' It was one of his many qualities.

'You slapped me!' I said, in case Mystery Man hadn't realised what he'd done.

'Indeed.' Mystery Man said. He looked me in the eye for a few seconds. I blinked, then winked. He shook his head and sighed again.

'I guess I'm stuck with you then,' he said quietly. He snapped into a more business-like mode, slapping his hands down on the table and standing up. I slapped my hands down as well and gave a few business-like nods. Altogether, it now felt like a sober, business-like atmosphere.

'What would you say,' said Mystery Man, 'If I told you that you were our number one murder suspect.'

I considered this. *Number one.* I had never won a prize before. Still, it was perhaps best to get a little more context.

'I would think I would say, "What do you mean?"'.

'Well, we caught you at the scene of the crime. Your fingerprints are all over the murder weapon. You assaulted several police officers.'

'Again, I must ask, what do you mean?'

'What part of this isn't clear? What can you not be getting?'

I sighed in a Mystery Man-ish fashion. Why was he being so obtuse?

'Who,' I said, talking slowly and pronouncing all my words clearly, 'has been murdered?'

Mystery Man looked at me balefully. 'I'm talking about Kenneth Keeble.'

I gave a baleful look of my own. 'I don't understand,' I said, not understanding.

Mystery Man slapped me on the side of the head again. Some people are ticking time bombs who can go off for no reason at any point. They are to be pitied, not feared.

'It's okay,' I said. Then, 'Wait, what? Kenneth's dead? What? What?'

'He had a large knife sticking out of his back. You were there. He's dead.'

This didn't tally with my version of events. 'But I mean, Mystery Man, I got the knife out.'

I spent the next little while or so screaming, 'No! Surely not!' and variations on that theme. Mystery Man sat watching and smoking cigarettes, his face occupying the exact mid-point between boredom and disgust. Kenneth was dead? *Dead*? This was a real shock. I had 100% not seen that one coming. Although, in retrospect, there were maybe some subtle clues I could have picked upon. Dead, though. Dead. Dead in a way it would be unreasonable

12

to refer to as 'alive'. Wow. Kenneth, my best and truest friend. Dead. Kenneth was dead and I was just going to have to get used to that fact.

I departed from the space under the table where I had been grieving and calmly resumed a seat opposite Mystery Man.

'Are you done now?' he said.

'Absolutely. I have mourned, now I am out on the other side.'

'Right then. So, actually I know you didn't kill Keeble. He was cold before you entered the building. The question is: who did?'

Solid question, no doubt about it. 'Who did?' I said.

'Exactly,' said Mystery Man. 'That's what we need to find out. And in doing so, I hope to take down one of the biggest criminals in the country.'

I nodded sagely and smiled. Mystery Man smiled and nodded.

'I have no idea what you're talking about,' I said.

Mystery Man's smile disappeared. 'Why did I have to get stuck with you?'

I had strong suspicions that this was what was known as a rhetorical question. Nevertheless, one could never be too careful.

'Dunno!' I said.

Mystery Man took something from his jacket pocket. It was a photo, a few years old, featuring a then-alive Kenneth smiling and holding a glass of champagne. With him were Donald, Sally and Hamish.

'Tell me everything you know about these three,' said Mystery Man.

I leaned back on my chair, put my feet up on the table and started to reminisce.

*

I was twenty years old and had been rejected three times from Glasgow University. As a born winner, this had of course not deterred me from attending lectures. Getting tutors to read my essays proved more problematic, even when I hand delivered them to their houses.

Those lectures. I shiver even now thinking about them. How fortunate our young minds were, to have the opportunity to be sculpted by the legendary, inestimable Professor Angus Pargus. A hero to every one of us, an icon of Scottish literature, responsible for classics such as *Hilda's Bath, Tenement Testament,* and of course, his masterpiece, *Potatoes On Sunday*.

His oratory style was something to behold. He would arrive half an hour after the lecture was due to begin and would generally not acknowledge the three hundred students in front of him for the first ten minutes. Then, he would pick someone at random and quiz them on various aspects of literature, punctuating their responses with barely concealed laughter and murmurs of 'idiotic,' and 'incredibly idiotic.' Quite a few cried. We all loved him.

In the main Professor Pargus shunned contact with students and staff outside of working hours. There were however a select group with whom he was occasionally seen in conversation. Such was my admiration for the man, I resolved to go to any lengths to be a part of this coterie: Kenneth, Donald, Sally and Hamish - they were Professor Pargus's Chosen Few.

Well, as it turns out, joining a closely knit friendship circle centred on a relationship with a legendary but opaque author is not as easy as one might think. Nevertheless, through a strict regimen

16

of frantic waving, sitting beside them and repeatedly introducing myself, in just a few short months each one of them knew my face. Our friendship hasn't greatly altered since – I'll start chatting, some sort of verbal or physical assault will take place, then I'll see what another member of the crew is up to. People like to say that change is important, but personally I enjoy the feeling of continuity whenever I hang with the old gang.

Donald Danworthy. Perhaps one of the greatest golfers Scotland has produced. The finer points of the sport remain a mystery to a non-player like me, but even I could appreciate the beauty and style with which he hit the small round object with the stick-type apparatus. Donald was infamous for his short temper on the course. Once, during the Open he dove into the crowd to attack an audience member who was continually shouting, 'You hit that ball, Donald!' each time he took a shot. To this day, my shoulder still hurts during the winter months from his club connecting with it.

17

Sadly, Donald's rage was to prove the cause of his enforced retirement at the age of twenty seven. After five terrible rounds in a row, he swung his club wildly in anger. Unluckily, it connected with his knee with the kind of power from which he had made a career. With his left leg pretty much out of commission, his days on the professional tour came to an end. Soon afterwards I recall suggesting to him that as he no longer needed all his clubs it might be an idea to transform some of them into a snazzy array of customised walking sticks. This innocuous remark earned me another blow to the shoulder.

I have always been a little in awe of Sally Sang. In university I would look at her at lunchtimes until she said, 'Stop looking at me'. Even then I would still gaze at her reflection in the back of my spoon, not caring how weirdly large it made her head look. A lovely head it was, surrounded by long brown hair that would elegantly fall over her face when she was laughing or shouting at me.

Art was always Sally's passion. I remember her first show at university. It featured recreations of famous sculptures with Sally's face affixed somewhere on each of them. There was a stir when Professor Pargus showed up, with whispers that it was the first non-mandatory university event he had attended in his twenty year tenure. He bought Sally's recreation of the Venus De Milo for an astonishingly large amount of money. Sally was so happy she started drinking an exceptional amount of wine and capped off the evening by extravagantly vomiting. It was the first of many such nights for Sally, who, in part due to the patronage of Professor Pargus, went on to become an internationally successful artist.

Kenneth and Hamish both maintained steady contact with Professor Pargus after leaving university. Kenneth worked in publishing and had edited the Professor's last five novels, including his latest, the disastrously received *Journey of The Space Ferret*.

Hamish Harrington on the other hand, well, I'd never been quite sure what he did for Professor Pargus. After university he disappeared for a few years and returned sporting a moustache and a hitherto unknown passion for ivory cufflinks. I had always felt a certain kinship with Hamish. Of the group, he was the one who was most likely to acknowledge my presence and engage in some form of conversation. Yes, back then I would have considered Hamish to be my closest friend. That made it all the more surprising that he tried to frame me for credit card fraud.

Eight stolen credit cards had been found in his possession. He was willing to testify under oath that I had given them to him and threatened his family if he told anyone. Looking back at the incident now, of course I can laugh, but at the time it was daunting. Eventually, due to a lack of evidence, the charges against me were dropped, but if I'm blunt, my feelings were a little hurt by the whole episode. When I mentioned this, Hamish laughed warmly and put an arm over my shoulders. 'Well, Cudgel,' he said,

'Obviously, I stole the cards, but getting caught is the kind of thing that lands a man in jail. To be honest, I just didn't fancy it. And I knew you're always game for helping a chap out.'

It was hard to argue with that logic. That said, if Hamish wanted to me to go to jail for him he should have told me. It's not good for friends to keep secrets from one another. Soon after that, he disappeared. Since his return he'd been working for Professor Pargus in some capacity.

'And that's pretty much all I know about them,' I said to Mystery Man.

'I see,' said Mystery Man, pacing around the cell. He lit another cigarette. I was beginning to think he might have a smoking problem.

'What you've told me confirms what I've suspected for years; Pargus has a close knit group of confidantes. That's how he's so slippery. That's how he never gets caught.'

There were several parts of this statement that I didn't understand. I started with the most pressing. 'Um, I'm pretty sure if Professor Pargus had a close knit group of confidantes I would be involved in it.'

Mystery Man took several long drags on his cigarette. It was honestly like he didn't know how bad smoking was for you. 'There's something I have to tell you about Professor Pargus. God knows, I can't believe it's you I have to tell, but you're the only one with the kind of access I need.'

I gave him a sceptical look. There was nothing he could tell me about Professor Pargus I didn't already know. The man was a hero to me.

Mystery Man said, 'Angus Pargus is arguably the most powerful and dangerous criminal in the country.'

22

It took a few seconds, five minutes at most, to understand what he had just said. Clearly I then had some questions. 'Eh?' I said.

'That's right,' said Mystery Man. 'Drugs, firearms, possibly even murder. The reclusive author thing is just a front.'

This didn't really chime with everything in my life I'd ever held dear to me. 'I don't believe it.' I said. 'I can't believe it.'

'It's true,' said Mystery Man

'Okay, I believe you.'

Mystery Man then proceeded to fill me in on the unsavoury elements of Professor Pargus's criminal empire. He was of the opinion that all of the group, including Donald and Sally were intimately bound up in the Professor's nefarious activities.

'So,' said Mystery Man, 'Kenneth's murder will have them all feeling pretty nervous. If Pargus can off him, he can off any of them. That's presuming, of course it wasn't one of them that did it.'

I burst out in hearty laughter. It was one thing to tell me that my longstanding hero was actually an evil criminal mastermind, it was another to say that one of my best friends was capable of murder.

'We can't rule anything out at this stage,' said Mystery Man.

I stopped laughing. I hadn't thought of it that way.

Mystery Man stubbed out his cigarette, and looked nervously at the door. 'Pargus is unbelievably powerful. He's got influence everywhere, including the police.'

This was perhaps the biggest surprise of all. Professor Pargus had been notoriously scathing about the police force in his third novel, *Five Hail Marys for Fergal.*

'That's why,' said Mystery Man with some difficulty, 'I need your help.'

'Ooh,' I said, enthralled.

'Danworthy, Sang and Harrington will be feeling vulnerable right now. They won't be able to trust each other. This is my one chance to get them to turn on each other and finally on Pargus. This is a chance to bring him to justice. I need you to talk each of them in turn, find out what they know, get a sense of how they're feeling, what they know about Kenneth's death.'

'You want me to investigate my friends for you?'

'I don't want to have to rely on you. But I have to rely on you. I can't trust the force.'

25

It was a tough call. There was so much to take in. I loved Donald, Sally and Hamish. We were compadres, amigos. Good God, they were like *family* to me. That said, you can't beat an adventure. 'Sounds good!' I said.

*

I made sure to get up early the next day, around 1am. When a seismic event is looming, it's vital to get a jump start on the rest of humanity. In a flurry, I brushed my teeth, showered, dressed, ate breakfast, and prepared some sandwiches. My efficiency in these mundane but crucial tasks meant I had a spare ten hours to kill before my first mission commenced. I clicked my tongue until it got annoying. What to do? There was probably something on television, but it seemed likely my neighbours would have drawn their curtains by now.

I sat on the couch. I stood up. And sat down. Then up once more. I knew I was being indecisive. Maybe it was nerves getting to me. Still, I sat and stood up. My knees began to tire and interesting colours appeared before my eyes. Transfixing as their beauty was, I knew I had to make a decision. Between standing up and sitting down. Between action and inaction. Wasn't this, in microcosm, the essential human dilemma? To do or not to do. And yet, by alternating between both I was in reality only achieving the latter. It was then that I knew that thought was a Trojan horse; that the consideration of whether to engage or not was itself a form of disengagement. Let me tell you, this felt like a hell of a revelation to come up with at two o'clock in the morning. That was that then; I was going to give myself a haircut.

Sadly, while my mind was now clear of everything but the task in hand, my body was not so up to speed. Maybe it was fighting all those policemen. Maybe it was that I'd only slept for an hour and half in the past two days. What I do know is that I collapsed and banged my head on the coffee table. As unconsciousness gripped I was fully aware of the irony that coffee was designed to keep one awake and alert. 'What crazy irony!' was my final thought.

I awoke thirteen hours later; Donald would already be on the golf course.

Despite his premature retirement, Donald still spent most mornings, afternoons and early evenings at his golf club, staying later if there was a function to attend. His wife Susan must have had a similarly hectic social schedule, for they were rarely seen together. There was a running joke around the club that this was because they led entirely separate lives and detested one another, that Donald was prone to drinking himself into a stupor before making uncalled for advances on clubhouse waitresses. What made the joke funnier was the drily grave demeanour people would adopt as they told it. Who would have thought a stuffy golf club in a scenic part of Scotland would contain so many deadpan comics? Great art can flourish anywhere, I suppose.

Though his bad leg rendered him unable to reach the astonishing levels of his prime, Donald nonetheless limped round the greens every day. The freedom afforded by retirement had led to him adding some quirks to his play. In his professional days he was famous for spending a punishing amount of time on each shot, weighing up the pros and cons before making an informed decision on the correct course of action. These days he tended to swing as soon as he was in immediate vicinity of the ball. Some time ago he had made the unorthodox call to carry a bottle of vodka with him round the course. Setting it carefully down beside him he would thwack violently at the ball until he either made contact or fell over. The time this took seemed to a layman like me to be inversely proportional to the amount of vodka left in the bottle. But then, what did I know about golf? When a successful shot was eventually struck, Donald would grin that famous Masters winning grin and shout, 'Take that, Susan!' in tribute to his wife.

Of course, eighteen holes is a long way to walk every day for a man with only one fully functioning leg. Unfortunately, Donald's golf cart usage had been restricted since the tree incident three summers ago. Now, he was only allowed on a cart as a passenger. Depending on how much vodka he had gotten through, this would not deter him from gamely attempting to shove his driver from the moving cart and driving into the distance, laughing and screaming something along the lines of, 'I'm free now, Susan! Riding off into the sunset!' The security team would generally let him ride around for an hour so before sending someone out to get him. It was touches of class like this that made the club what it was.

I took up my usual perch at the fifteenth (fifty yards from the green, behind the barbed wire) and waited for Donald to appear. Despite my regular presence both here and at the club's entrance, it had been a year since Donald and I had spoken. I took a bite of sandwich. Getting Donald to talk about Professor Pargus and Kenneth would be tricky. He might still be mourning. I was glad I had made so many sandwiches. Maybe I could offer one to Donald to get him to open up. I was sure he enjoyed sandwiches. God, who doesn't?

As I chewed thoughtfully and began to map out a post-sandwich offer strategy I became aware of a presence lurking behind me. Turning round revealed a young gentleman of about ten years of age, clad in golf club blazer and regarding me with an air of total disdain.

'What are you doing here?' said the young gentleman.'

Never had I heard such a nuanced expression of contempt packed into just five short words. A slight pause for emphasis after the 'what' segued into a relatively neutral 'are'. It was when he reached 'you' that he began to make his feelings clear. Long and

31

drawn out, accessorised with a slight yet perceptible roll of the eyes that inferred he considered my presence to be a personal affront, and that there was nothing I could say that would change that.

By comparison, 'doing' was relatively sedate, but still seemed to hint at some form of wayward untowardness on my part. It was a suggestive 'doing', implying there was no limit to the level of gruesome awfulness he caught me partaking in.

The 'here' was interesting. Like the 'you' it was an audio and visual experience. As he launched into the 'h' he swept his hand theatrically around him, landing it nonchalantly in his pocket by the end of '-ere'. The literal *here* to which he was referring seemed double-edged. It initially seemed to call back to the baffled disgust of the 'doing' era. On closer inspection though, it encompassed a much wider scope than merely *here*, i.e. beside the barbed wire at the fifteenth. He was really questioning why I was in proximity to the club itself. He knew I was not a member and that I didn't own a fancy embroidered blazer. With 'here', the young

gentleman was gazing into my very soul and was disgusted by what

he saw.

'What are *you* doing here?' I retorted straightforwardly.

Normally I am a kindly sort to anyone smaller than me, but I was in

no mood to divulge my plans to a fancy coated little snob. I took

large bite of sandwich to indicate I no longer wished to speak to

him.

'My father owns this place. I can have you thrown out.'

Being no stranger to intimidation and intimations of getting thrown

out of places, I knew where I stood, both figuratively and literally.

I swallowed my mouthful of sandwich. 'This is public

property. I have as much right to be here as you.'

After considering this, the young gentleman took the

unexpected course of action of launching headfirst at me. His skull met my stomach with some force and he commenced kicking, punching and generally attacking me. This was a tricky predicament. How is one meant to react to an attack by such a small human being? My first thought was to hope he eventually tired himself out, but as the seconds wore on he seemed only to be increasing in strength. Eventually, after backing into the barbed wire and receiving several small cuts to the back of the neck I could take no more. With a heavy heart I lifted my arm, bag of sandwiches and all, and gave the young gentleman a light shove.

He stumbled back a few steps and looked at me with something approaching awe.

'How…how *dare you*,' he hissed. I wouldn't consider myself a religious man, but I could swear at that moment I could see the shadow of Satan darken his eyes.

In one abrupt move, the young gentleman punched me a final time in the gut and ran away. As I doubled over, pain mingling with relief that the ordeal had ended, I heard a familiar stream of expletives carry over the calm afternoon air.

'Take that, Susan!' Donald had reached the fifteenth.

*

After a clinical mixture of cajoling, crying and refusing to let go of his arm, Donald had agreed to have a drink with me. It was only as we sat opposite one another in the clubhouse that I had a good opportunity to look at his face. It's always seemed to me that one can tell a lot about a man from his face; whether he is awake or sleeping, the dimensions of his nose etc. It is – in most circumstances – the most instinctive part of one's body. People may lie with their mouths, in their faces lie only truth. At least to me. It's not an exact science, but I'd wager that around 40% of the time, I can tell what someone is thinking merely by looking at their face. It's a gift.

Donald's face did not look great. The chin, in his prime coated with a layer of dark stubble that hinted at a bold virility, was now clothed by a fluffy, dropping beard spattered with disrespectful tufts of grey. His eyes, once as cruel and searching as a hawk with a chip on its shoulder and an overabundance of lunch options, were now hazy and half shut. We had been sitting for ten minutes and Donald was on his fourth Bloody Mary.

'What the hell do you want then, Cudgel?' he said, speaking to me for the first time since we sat down.

This was tricky. How does one ask a friend if they've murdered another friend? As well as this, I'd have to get his thoughts on the whole Professor Pargus being a master criminal thing. Good lord, this was an onerous task Mystery Man had set me. I remembered the advice he had given me before we had parted, those sage words of wisdom that must have been passed

36

from generation to generation, one Mystery Man to another, a hidden knowledge imparted: 'Just please don't be an idiot.'

I tried in vain to catch Donald's eye as he searched for Lisa the waitress.

'Donald, let's talk about Kenneth, who was shockingly murdered yesterday. Thoughts?' I said.

Donald belched. After licking the inside of his glass he belched again, more forcefully this time. Lisa the waitress reached our table. The thought occurred that Donald may not have been paying attention to me.

'Lisa, we meet again.' Donald said.

'A Bloody Mary, Mr Danworthy?'

'Damn right. A Bloody Mary. *Mary*, what was her game, eh?…Lisa, I'd like a Bloody Mary.'

'Coming right up,' said Lisa the waitress.

'Hurrying away? Stay a while. Haven't even asked my friend here if he wants one.'

Lisa turned to me, rolling her eyes in a manner I had never witnessed without being the cause. 'One for you as well?'

Of course I was well aware that I was in the clubhouse to do a job. Mystery Man was relying on me. He had placed his trust in me and only me. I was morally bound to fulfil the task he had set me. That *said*, there I was, sitting in the clubhouse in front of everybody, Donald Danworthy calling me his *friend*, Lisa the waitress looking at me with non-disdain in her eyes. The effect was as intoxicating as I imagined four Bloody Marys in ten minutes to be.

'Yes, a Bloody Mary for me too, Lisa the waitress. The bloodiest you have, haha!'

'Right,' said Lisa, leaving us.

'Good old Lisa,' I said.

'Old? Unlikely,' said Donald. 'Twenty one if she's a day. Fine age. All as it should be. Not old and bitter. Not like some people.'

Donald's volume was starting to increase. It was a delicate moment. From the way his eyes had stared at the undone button on Lisa's blouse to his words now, it started to occur to me that what people said about his marriage to Susan may not have merely been a several hundred strong in-joke. Nonetheless, if after finishing my Bloody Mary I was to get the info I needed, it was imperative to keep him as on-topic as possible. But maybe he wasn't talking about Susan at all and I was just being a big silly. Yes, my face reading skills are prodigious, but words, with all their connotations and inflections, can sometimes get the better of me.

'To be clear,' I said, 'when you say "old and bitter", are you talking about Susan? Your wife Susan? That's she's old and bitter? Susan, I mean? But that Lisa isn't? Is that right?'

If my aim here was to get to the root of what was Donald was saying and for everything to be out in the open then yes, it's fair to say I succeeded. However, given that my overarching goal was to then gracefully steer the conversation away from Donald's marriage, I would have to admit that I had somewhat erred.

Donald thumped the table, 'I hate her! Oh God I hate her so much!'

'Susan, you mean?' I said.

Donald banged the table with such force the bread rolls jumped. 'Marriage. *Marriage.* I'll tell you something about marriage, Cudgel. A little something. This is all you have to know…this is what people *need* to know-…'

Before Donald could finish his anecdote, Lisa arrived with our drinks. It was my first ever Bloody Mary and I'd be lying if I said I wasn't excited. I took a good slug. It was *horrible*, like someone had defiled a perfectly good tomato then guiltily left it in the cupboard for a month.

'Lisa,' said Donald. 'Lisa, Lisa, Lisa, Lisa. What's it all about, Lisa? All of it?'

'I don't know, Mr Danworthy.'

'Mmm. How's it going, Lisa?'

'It's going fine. Enjoy your drinks.'

'No, Lisa. I said, how's it *going*?'

In one deft movement that recalled his youthful athleticism, Donald downed his drink. Simultaneously, with his free hand he grabbed the back of Lisa's blouse and pulled her towards him.

'How's it going?' Donald said again. It was starting to become something of a catchphrase.

Lisa, by a distance the younger of the pair, wasn't to be outdone for nimbleness. As soon as Donald got hold of her, she performed a kind of slick pirouette. With one of her hands she grabbed Donald's wrist while the other took hold of his fingers. Gracefully, she twisted the wrist one way whilst holding his middle finger in position. There followed an interesting popping sound and then an even more interesting yelping noise from Donald.

Lisa gazed down at her handiwork. 'Careful with the drinks, Mr Danworthy. Don't want to ruin your golf game.' With that she turned to serve another table. All in all, an impressive cameo.

Donald looked sadly at his finger, now bent curiously at a forty five degree angle to his other digits. He looked back over at Lisa, as she took another patron's order with a smile. 'That used to

42

work,' he said. For the first time he looked me directly in the eye. 'You remember me in my prime, Cudgel?'

Of course I did. And he had been magnificent. Telling him so appeared to be the right thing to do. And yet, by doing so I would be confirming that his prime was now firmly rooted in the past. And *yet*, by asking me this question it seemed that Donald was aware his prime had passed. Unless, his question was a bluff and he was desperate for assurance he still in the middle of a healthy prime with plenty of longevity left in it. All told, it was best to play it safe.

'Would you like to talk some more about Susan?' I said.

This time, Donald chose not to make solid contact with the table with his fists. Instead he breathed deeply and slouched on his chair, his wavering eyes achieving resolution and shutting. For a moment, I thought he might be dead. What awful luck it would have been to have two close friends die within the space of twenty

four hours.

Thankfully, a grunting, vaguely angry sound began to

emanate from him, informing me that he was merely asleep. Whilst

a sleeping Donald was on the whole preferable to a dead one, he

was still not much use for the task in hand. I cursed myself for

having been so easily side-tracked by bonhomie and disgusting red

drinks. There's a time and a place for everything and I still hadn't

asked Donald if he had murdered Kenneth yesterday or if he

happened to know who else might have.

Coiling my forefinger behind my thumb in anticipation I

leaned towards him. Up close his haggard face appeared softer,

almost cherubic. One swift flick to the nostril would be enough.

Hesitating a few inches from his face, the gravity of the

moment hit me; I had never intentionally inflicted physical

violence on a friend before. Was it worth it? Donald's Bloody

44

Mary breath and idiosyncratic body odour filled my nose and clouded my mind. Leaning over the table was very uncomfortable and my legs began to shake.

No. *No*. This had to be done. For the greater good. For Mystery Man. For Kenneth. Taking a deep breath, I steadied my hand in front of his nose and flicked with all my might.

In the milliseconds before I made a connection, Donald woke up. I'd have to imagine he probably wasn't expecting my face to be inches from his, much less my forefinger to be heading for a direct hit on his nose. Therefore, I guess he can be forgiven for catching my finger in his mouth and clamping down hard with tomato stained teeth.

Normally, there's nothing I like less than causing a scene. I prefer to be an observer rather than a participant in any drama or scandal. So it gave me absolutely no pleasure to have to scream loudly in the middle of a busy clubhouse, 'Oh God no! My finger! Please God no!'

I tried pulling away, but Donald seemed in no mind to let go. Honestly, what were they putting in those Bloody Marys? I pulled again, still Donald gave no quarter. This odd game of tug of war continued for a spell.

It occurred to me that with Donald in such a tomato-red mist I could be in danger of losing my finger to his toothy clutches. As a keen fan of all my digits, this really wasn't on. I did some quick reasoning; my intended flick hadn't actually met its target, so I was still technically due at least one act of violence to resolve the situation.

With my other hand I swung at Donald with all my might, catching him hard on the left ear. Immediately, it had the desired effect; my finger was freed as Donald stared open mouthed in shock.

'I'm very sorry,' I said.

Donald didn't respond, at least not verbally. Instead, he mirrored me with a punch of his own. Now, as mentioned, Donald had imbibed several drinks by this stage, and thus his swing was not the fastest. Had I been inclined, I daresay I could have moved out of the way. However, it seemed important to restore equilibrium and equality to our relationship. I had punched him, and now it was his turn. Fair's fair.

He got me on the right temple. Speaking as someone who has been punched a great many times in their life I've become something of a connoisseur. It was not that I didn't respect Donald's punch – given the circumstances it was a game effort – but it certainly did not have the wow factor of punches past. It didn't knock me off my feet.

This could partly be explained by Donald electing to punch with the hand Lisa the waitress had only recently mangled. Thus,

47

when fist connected with face, it was he who gasped and crumpled to the ground. Poor Donald, it hadn't been a great five minutes for him.

Just as I was debating whether he would view my offer of a hand back to his feet as a veiled mockery, there appeared a vision that cooled my blood: the young gentleman had entered the clubhouse.

What to do? My first reaction was to hide for a while and hope that everything would turn out okay. It wasn't that I was scared of the young gentleman per se, more that I was wary of the clout he may have possessed at the club. As a rule, youngsters weren't allowed in the clubhouse unless they had serious connections. Maybe his father really did run the place.

It seemed that I had two options. Sit on the floor beside Donald or stay exactly where I was and hope that the young gentleman didn't notice me. The former was tricky – Donald and I *had* just been engaged in hand to hand combat, after all.

That really only left the doing-nothing-and-hoping-for-the-best gambit. It was all I had. I stayed rooted to the spot and stared intently at a painting on the wall of a lady on a horse. The lady was wearing a red dress. A lovely dress it was, and the lady looked lovely as well. This is not to downplay the loveliness of the horse. It was magnificent, brown and horse-like. A fantastic painting, all things considered.

I was wondering if there was any possible way I could get a closer look at the thing when I noticed a tapping sensation on my shoulder. I turned to see a short person in front of me. Not as short as the young gentleman but certainly smaller than me. By exactly how much I couldn't say – it didn't seem the time to suggest standing back to back. He was wearing a fetching white jacket and black trousers combination. I fancied he was the clubhouse manager and told him as much.

'That is correct,' said the clubhouse manager. 'I am afraid I shall have to ask you and Mr Danworthy to leave.'

He had a foreign accent, yet also spoke the English language perfectly, with a beautiful mellifluous quality. I was not unimpressed.

'Great to hear,' I complimented him.

'If you would kindly escort yourself and Mr Danworthy outside.'

This wasn't so bad. Obviously, I had been asked to leave a number of establishments in the past. At least on this occasion I would be accompanied by a friend. There was even the chance that being ejected together would further strengthen the bond between Donald and I. With any luck he would feel comfortable telling me all about Professor Pargus's criminal activity and if he had happened to stab Kenneth. Really, the clubhouse manager had done me a tremendous favour. I leaned down and kissed his shiny forehead.

From my vantage point just north of his perfectly coiffed hair I was struck by a terrifying sight. The young gentleman was staring directly into my eyes.

As outlined previously, on my day I can be quite the face reader. When the young gentleman's eyes met mine I felt a sense of understanding. The kerfuffle by the barbed wire was now firmly in the past. It was not the start of a long-lasting and destructive enmity, rather a slight miss-step on what would surely become a productive friendship. I've always wanted to be a mentor to someone, here was my chance.

The young gentleman picked up a fork from a nearby table and charged towards me. It was a surprising development that made me question whether I may have over-estimated my face

reading skills. Either that or the young gentleman was not human

and was actually some form of inscrutable demonic creature.

Frankly, from his crazed smile as he headed nearer it was hard to

tell what was more plausible.

The clubhouse manager, hearing the young gentleman's

manic wail grow louder as he approached seemed to deduce there

was no stopping him. In recognition of this, he adroitly hopped out

of the way and calmly hid under the nearest table. It looked like a

practiced manoeuvre and made me wonder if such fork-wielding

rampages were a regular occurrence. That was really the kind of

thing that should be mentioned in the brochure.

With the clubhouse manager gone, the young gentleman

had a clear run at me. Certainly I didn't want to fight him – I am no

bully. That said, he clearly was intending to stab me with a fork,

possibly multiple times. He drew closer, glee on his face, fork glinting as he held it high. Ready to strike. I lifted Donald from the ground and used him as a rudimentary shield. The young gentleman brought his weapon forth, getting Donald just above the left knee.

Some words of explanation are probably in order. Yes, I allowed my friend to be stabbed with a fork instead of me. Of course I felt awful about it. It pained me like a fork to the leg. But it absolutely had to be done. Mystery Man had entrusted me with a job. For all I knew, Professor Pargus might be planning a hit on Donald. There was a chance that by letting him get stabbed, I was saving Donald's life.

'Gideon!' said a woman in a pale orange dress as she entered the room. 'Did you just stab *another* club member?'

The young gentleman bowed his head, chastened. He looked down at Donald, who had resumed his berth on the ground.

'Sorry,' mumbled the young gentleman. Dropping the fork, he slouched over to the woman, who had to be his mother. She began to reprimand him and soon the young gentleman was in tears. This in turn caused his mother to cry and she immediately promised him some ice cream. With that they left the room.

Donald had looked better. A broken finger, a punch to the face and a fork to the leg were probably not what he had expected from a day at the club. He was so utterly defeated that he didn't even fight back when I hauled him to his feet and started dragging him out of the clubhouse. Somewhat fortunately, the forking hadn't been on Donald's bad leg, sparing him any further pain in that body part. This meant that his normally sturdy left leg was now bleeding profusely. As a result, walking – even with my support – proved difficult, and he collapsed to the floor, where, it must be said, he had spent quite a bit of time recently.

I lifted him again, really putting my back into it. And then suddenly, we were moving together as one. After a few seconds of marvelling at my hitherto untapped brawn I realised the clubhouse manager had also taken hold of Donald and that we were escorting him out as team.

With a short glance of principled disgust, the clubhouse manager left us as soon as we got outside. The chill night air roused Donald. He pushed me weakly aside. It was now or never.

'Donald, I need to know what happened to Kenneth. What did Professor Pargus have to do with it?'

Donald ignored me, and with a great deal of effort, and in only six attempts, made it to his feet. While delighted for him, he still hadn't answered my question.

'Donald!' I said again, panic creeping into my voice as he moved very, very, very slowly away from me. 'Who killed Kenneth?'

Still, he continued glacially. There was nothing else for it. My cardinal rule had already been smashed tonight. In for a penny, in for a pound. I moved over to Donald, and with a swift swipe of my left foot I took his legs from underneath him. Yet again, Donald was on the ground.

'Talk to me, Donald. Talk to me!'

He groaned, turned his head, and began to crawl away.

'I don't want to inflict any more pain on you!' I said, alarmed.

Donald looked back at me and wearily shook his head. 'You don't know anything, you idiot. This isn't pain compared to what would happen if I talked about the Professor.'

While part of me was keen to keep beating him until he cracked, I knew in my heart that would never happen. Professor Pargus certainly ran a strict organisation. I would have to return to

Mystery Man empty handed. Sighing, I sat on the steps and watched Donald crawl further and further until the night had swallowed him whole.

*

Mystery Man and I were hanging in a disused railway station. A mouse had run past us several times. Or maybe it was several different mice. It was going pretty fast and I don't pretend to be an expert.

'And then, what, you just let him crawl away?' said Mystery Man.

'I wouldn't say he's crawling. He's moving at a fair speed. Plus for all we know it could be a girl.'

'What the hell are you talking about? Danworthy – you just let him get away without asking anything else?'

I had come to our rendezvous armed with my first ever flask of coffee. Even after my third cup, I had yet to develop a taste for it. I took another gulp and shuddered. 'Bah.'

'Stop saying "bah". We also have a room of witnesses saying you beat the crap out of Danworthy.'

'Bah. That's a gross mischaracterisation of the facts.'

'I don't care. Do you know the strings I had to pull to cover it up? I can't have the other detectives getting suspicious.' Mystery Man started pacing round in circles along the platform.

'You're like a caged tiger!' I said.

'You need to understand how dangerous Pargus is. Do you get that?'

'He once threw a copy of *Jane Eyre* at me because I didn't like the poltergeist thing.'

58

Mystery Man frowned. 'Five years I've been working on this. Five years waiting for a way in. Now a domino has fallen. This is the best chance yet to finally get near to Pargus.'

'Is Kenneth the domino in this scenario?'

'For the first time, Sang, Danworthy and Harrington will be watching their backs. They'll be worried. A cornered beast is a dangerous beast.'

I thought about this. 'Like a caged tiger!'

'Since they'll be thinking they could be offed at any time, they might feel a bit more inclined to talk.'

I sipped at my coffee. 'Bah,' I said thoughtfully.

'Now, Danworthy is a drunken wreck, so he probably wouldn't have been much use anyway. But you're going to see Sang next and she for sure knows things.'

Sally. Sally, Sally, Sally, Sally. I closed my eyes, thinking of her lovely hair, her lovely eyes and lovely skin. Sally.

'Wake up!' said Mystery Man. 'So, you'll visit her tomorrow.'

'Indeed!'

Mystery Man rubbed his face. '*Try* not to be so stupid.'

The mouse ran past us again. In a bid to impress Mystery Man I dived after it, but alas, it was too fast for me and I was left with nothing but two scraped palms and the sight of Mystery Man's feet as he walked away.

*

If I was to be seeing Sally it was imperative that I looked at my best. A new pair of trousers were in order. I understood there to be several places selling such wares in town. All that required was that I visit each of these establishments, have a detailed inspection

at the products on offer, comparing and contrasting aspects such as

price and quality, and then finally, after giving everything a good

mull over, purchase a pair of trousers. It made me laugh to think

some people could over-complicate a simple task like shopping for

clothes.

To prove my point, the instant I walked into the first trouser

outlet I saw them. Luminous green with a blue and red zigzag

cheekily corralling down each leg. Without question, they were the

finest pair of trousers I had ever seen.

'I must possess you,' I said to the trousers and began

extricating them from the mannequin.

'Sir. Sir!' A woman with a name badge reading 'Pam'

approached me. 'You can't take them off the dummy like that.'

I love a challenge and Pam's good natured dare made me

move at double speed. Soon I was in the changing room, carefully removing my shoes and exultantly trying on the trousers. They looked better than I could have dreamed. I twirled coquettishly in the mirror then looked disdainfully at my old trousers. There they lay, looking old and stupid like a pair of less impressive trousers. With nary another glance I left them behind and strutted to the checkout.

'These, please,' I said, slamming my wallet down. 'Take as much as you want.'

Striding out of the store I heard a little boy remark to his mother, 'Why is that man wearing women's trousers?' I didn't even bother to turn and look. Even if there was some man who definitely wasn't me wearing women's trousers I didn't care. I looked fantastic. Sally would be into these trousers, no doubt about it.

One other, odd detail from the day. As I sat in a café afterwards, wearing my excellent trousers and wondering whether I wanted a bacon roll, a roll and sausage or perhaps some unheralded combination of the two, I noticed a man was staring at me. He was a large fellow with a large shaved head, upon which a large scar featured prominently. Our eyes met briefly across the café then he returned to his newspaper like he hadn't just been staring directly at me. This happened at few more times over the course of my bacon roll and sausage. I considered going over to say hello but what with the prospect of seeing Sally the next day as well as all of the stuff happening with Mystery Man and Kenneth being murdered and Professor Pargus turning out to be a master criminal I decided that the best thing to do was to ignore the large fellow for the time being. If we were meant to be friends then fate would surely throw us back together at some point.

The next day I awoke with a smile on my face. What a day it promised to be. I cleaned my teeth with gum-bleeding vigour and showered until my skin was pink and my fingers crinkled. With a certain ceremony I put on the trousers. Now, normally I'm not one for aftershave but today it felt appropriate. Wanting to be efficient I decided it could also be used for slicking back my hair. The aroma was intoxicating, and to be honest, a little overwhelming. I had to sit down for a moment.

Sally had never wavered in her commitment to the artistic, bohemian lifestyle. After the monumental success of her third exhibition, *Sally: It's About Me: Sally*, I had wondered whether extreme wealth would change her. My fears were unfounded. She still lived in the same old tenement as she had through university, the only difference being that she now owned the entire building, leasing out rooms to her artist comrades. Such was her humility that aside from the forty foot mural of her face that adorned the front of the building, it was impossible to tell that it was the residence of a world famous artist.

In keeping with her utopian ideal, Sally had ensured that outside of her quarters all doors in the building remained unlocked at all times. I entered the close and clambered over the usual mix of tired alcoholics and creative types that gave the place its distinctive character and odour.

Sally occupied the entire top floor herself. It was only as I reached the summit that I realised how nervous I was. I breathed deeply and tried to move my left hand to knock the door. Nothing. I tried again, no dice. I gave it a go with my right but there was nothing doing. I breathed deeper and tried both hands simultaneously. Still I couldn't knock the blasted door. Deeper yet I breathed. It was becoming a wheeze.

'George,' said a voice from the other side of the door, 'Are you having another heart attack? Remember I told you to let me film it.'

Sally's voice. I was so close. Since my hands had clearly failed me there was nothing else for it. The door needed knocked. I tilted back, then, with some amount of force, launched my head forwards.

It was an unfortunate moment for Sally to open the door. Too late to recant my head's trajectory, all I could do was try and ease the force a little.

'Jesus Christ!'

'I'm sorry!'

'You headbutted me!'

'My hands…they wouldn't knock.'

'Right on the nose. Is it bleeding?'

It was bleeding. Quite a bit, actually.

'No. It isn't.'

Sally looked in a mirror. 'That's a lot of blood.'

'Ah. Well. Yes, I suppose it is bleeding. Hahaha,' I laughed nervously to ease the tension. Was it my lot in life to constantly injure the ones I love? I hadn't thought so, but the evidence was really beginning to stack up.

Sally gazed at herself in the mirror, not saying anything. The silence began to feel somewhat awkward. I started to hum. Sally dabbed a finger to her nose then wiped the blood on her forehead. I hummed a bit louder. She wiped some blood across her cheeks and looked at me. My humming ceased.

'Stay there,' she said and dashed into another room. She returned seconds later with an old fashioned looking camera. 'Take my picture,' she said. I hesitated for a moment to ensure she was talking to me. 'Come on,' she said.

I held the camera in fumbling hands. There was a big button on the side I assumed would perform the primary function. I aimed in Sally's general direction and pressed down.

67

'Great stuff!' said Sally happily, 'I've been wondering how best to document my grief and here it is. Blood! I mean, *blood*, you know?'

I did not know. I started to hum again. Sally looked down and her eyes lit up.

'Look at your trousers! Jesus Christ!'

My heart swelled. *Exactly* the reaction I'd been hoping for. 'My trousers,' I confirmed, lest there be any doubt.

'Alright fine, come in,' Sally said.

I sat in Sally's living room, taking it all in. Save for the couch hanging upside down from the ceiling there were no chairs. The carpet though, was so incredibly luxurious and thick that this was no hardship. It was in fact so voluminous that getting back to one's feet appeared to present a real challenge. 'It's a whole new thing. We call it Quicksand,' Sally had explained when we entered. 'Haven't seen the cat in a while, though.'

Beyond the thicket of carpet, I was able to make out a man and woman in the corner of the room. They had matching short white hair and were dressed all in black. Both were slouched against the wall listlessly.

'That's Sam and Sam,' Sally had said. 'They're having an existential crisis.'

Male Sam yawned and Female Sam nodded towards me with a small smile.

Presently Sally was examining the fabric of my trousers. 'So ridiculous,' she muttered in awe. She sat back and lit a cigarette.

'I am heartbroken,' she said. 'With Kenneth dead my entire world is a mess. Life is a sham. I hate myself and everyone else.'

She took a long drag and exhaled through her nose. One of the cotton buds she had used to stem the bleeding popped out and was lost, possibly forever, to the carpet.

'Still, life goes on, eh! Plus I always thought something like this would happen. Kenneth was on some pretty thin ice with the Professor.'

Sally was talking about Professor Pargus! Mystery Man was going to be pleased. However, she didn't seem to have realised her bud had fallen out and her nose had started to bleed again. What a dilemma. On one hand, here was a chance to do exactly what had been asked of me and aid a clandestine investigation into a master criminal. On the other hand, no one likes to see their friend with a bleeding nose.

'One of your cotton buds has fallen out. You should go and replace it immediately'

'What? Oh, so it has. I'll go get a new one.'

With some difficulty, Sally extricated herself from the carpet and left the room.

'Hello,' I said to Sam and Sam.

'Hello,' said Female Sam. Male Sam yawned again.

Sally returned, new bud in place. 'Is this a good look?' she said, 'I'm going to a party later. I can't remember anyone else wearing buds before.' She looked at her watch. 'Still got a bit of time. So why exactly are you here?'

'Glad you asked.'

I had a ready response to this question. It was epic in scope and devastating in argument. There had been four drafts before I had been satisfied.

Through a mixture of jumping, scarping and rolling, I was able to stand up. Clearing my throat I began, 'Once upon a time…'

'You know, I wonder if your trousers would fit me.'

Once more, Sally was fixating on my trousers. Turns out there's such a thing as being too stylish. Normally, this would be a wonderful state of affairs but I was already locked into my speech. And now that I had got going I found I was unable to halt.

'I'd like to try them on,' said Sally.

'Machiavellian…' I continued apace, powerless to stop.

Sally looked very excited. 'Imagine, the buds and those trousers. It would be a whole new thing.'

'…Did I feel left out? Perhaps…'

Sally slithered along the carpet towards me. My speech still had nine minutes to run, and that didn't even include time factored in for applause. I needed to speed up my words per minute. 'You don't mind do you?' she said, grabbing a hem.

72

'…Phosphorescent…'

'So I'll just…'

'…Of which only four could be classed as sandwiches…

'You could give me hand you know…'

'…*He* maintained he thought it was a fire exit…'

'Nearly…'

'…So it's vital…'

'Stay *still*…'

'…that we talk about…'

'Finally!'

'Kenneth.'

I paused and took a deep breath. Sally held my fantastic trousers in her hands and sighed.

'This Kenneth thing. It's such a big mess.'

Using every ounce of willpower I could summon, I refrained from continuing into Act Two. In any case, I had forgotten my lute, which pretty much rendered the musical interlude obsolete. Instead I used the clever line Mystery Man had given me. 'Tell me about it.'

Sally sighed once more and lit another cigarette. I coughed gently, as ever politely disgusted by the habit.

'Do you want one?' she asked.

'Absolutely,' I said.

She handed me one and offered a lighter.

'I prefer mine unlit.' I said, immediately congratulating myself on coming up with such an excellent line.

'We were all so young,' said Sally, reclining back on the carpet until all I could see were the tops of her knees. 'And Professor Pargus, well, he's just so charismatic.'

I nodded vigorously. No one needed to tell me about the man's aura. It was palpable, like an excellent cologne.

'It started off small. Little things, to test us. Stealing, punching the occasional person in the face. Kid stuff, really.'

I bit down on my cigarette. It did not, as I'd hoped, contain chocolate.

Sally continued. 'After a while he knew we were his. We would have done anything for him. And that's when it got real.'

In the smoke filled room, hidden amongst the Quicksand carpet, my mind drifted into a liminal zone between the present and past, Sally's voice my guide. How well I could recall those heady university days and yet how little it appeared I had known. I had always thought of myself as part of the inner sanctum but it really was beginning to seem like that might not have been the case. I marvelled at what Sally was divulging. Having considered my perspective on events to be pretty much the definitive historical record, it was quite the trip to hear her detailing an experience that did not correspond precisely with mine. My head was a-swirl and I was sure it wasn't just due to the ever decreasing amount of oxygen in the room.

Sally was really getting into her stride. Maybe it was because she couldn't actually see me, but this was the longest conversation we'd ever had. 'Oh, but you have to realise how exciting it was!' she said. We were young and breaking the law. The *law*. Anything the Professor asked we would do. We were renegades. Drug deals, selling firearms, writing scathing reviews of his colleagues' novels under assumed names – *nothing* was off the table.'

A shade of sadness darkened Sally's tone and muddied the good vibes in the room. 'But after a while…it all became too much. There's only so much crime you can commit, I think. For me anyway. Plus, I had my career to think about. Donald, as well. You see, we were both starting to get well known. Donald especially felt that being in league with an international criminal might be bad for his golf game. That it could cost him some sponsorship deals down the line.'

'How did the Professor take you both leaving?' I said.

'He said he was fine with it, but I worry. My last three boyfriends have all died in motorcycle accidents, and I can't recall any of them actually owning a motorcycle. But maybe I'm just paranoid.'

'What about Hamish and Kenneth?'

Sally laughed, 'Hamish? Who can be sure, he's so slippery. He's the Professor's Number Two on the hidden illegal whatnots, I think. Kenneth was in charge of the public stuff, editing the Professor's novels. It was a well-run machine. At least until *Journey of the Space Ferret* came out.'

I shuddered at the mention of the dreaded novel's name. From the swaying of the carpet I could tell Sally had done the same.

'You think that's what got Kenneth killed?' I asked.

'Could be, I mean have you *read* it?'

I shuddered once more, remembering a twenty page long tangent into the biology and evolutionary process of the native Quaglorks.

'So where is Professor Pargus now?'

'Dunno, been a while since I've seen him. To be honest I'm a bit worried I could be bumped off next. You never know. But right now I imagine the Professor is holed up in that secret hideaway of his beside…hang on,' said Sally sitting upright. 'Why are you asking all these questions?'

I sunk further down into the carpet, so as to avoid having to lie to Sally's face. 'No reason,' I said. 'The police aren't involved.'

Her tone grew sharper, 'Cudgel, are you working for the police?'

Risking possible asphyxiation, I sunk even further. 'The police? Who? No. No, no, no. No.'

Sally clucked her tongue like a suspicious chicken. 'Hmm, I suppose it's unlikely that they'd ask *you* to help them.'

'Yeah, I guess...' I said, really not understanding why she'd say that.

'I can't believe I told you all that,' she said. 'It is a strange time, I suppose. What with the funeral tomorrow.'

'What's that?'

'Kenneth's funeral. It's tomorrow. Quite the occasion I imagine. Wish I could have designed the coffin,' she added wistfully.

Feeling a mite offended that no one had thought to invite me, I began the long process of standing up. Maybe everyone just assumed I already knew/organised the thing. That made the most sense.

Sally clapped her hands together in a forthright manner. 'I'd better get ready. Got to get my funeral outfit sorted before the party later. Could be a late one.' On that she left the room. After a while it occurred to me that she probably wasn't coming back. After another, longer while it occurred to me that I should be leaving.

'Lovely to meet you,' I said to both Sams as I waded out of the room.

'Bye,' they said in unison.

The long climb down the stairs did not seem nearly as daunting as the trip up. Nodding happily at the drunks drinking and writers reciting rhymes (and drinking), I congratulated myself on a job well done. I felt a tap on my shoulder as I reached the bottom. Turning round, I was surprised to see none other than Sam (female) standing before me.

'Yo,' I said. 'Where's Male Sam?'

She shook her head. She was small, but her eyes were wide and expressive, like she'd just figured out a particularly difficult crossword clue. She beckoned me towards her, looking round to make sure no one was listening.

'Loch Tryg,' she said portentously.

'Eh?' I said, portentously.

'That's where Professor Pargus's secret hideaway is,' she said. Then she ran back up the stairs.

It was then that it hit me: I wasn't wearing any trousers.

*

In a run of Big Days, this one was shaping up as potentially the Biggest. Kenneth's funeral. I mean, wow. I had wanted to purchase another pair of excellent trousers to rock up in, but annoyingly the outlet had not been open at 2am. My attempts to break in and take what I wanted also proved fruitless. Glass doors are sturdier than they look, and apparently don't get softened up no matter how often one runs into them.

Thus, I had acquiesced into wearing the black suit, white shirt and black tie that Mystery Man had provided. Whilst I suppose I looked handsome and magnificent, it could hardly be said to be the most fashion forward choice.

Mystery Man had sat me down and provided a detailed and comprehensive outline of the plan for the day, to which I had nodded along and yawned.

'Any questions?' he said, finishing up.

'So, I'm to be going to the funeral then?'

He slammed his hand down on the table and went through the plan again. This time my nods were more fervent and my yawns more tactically stifled behind my hands.

'Yes. *Yes*. I absolutely understand,' I said when he finished.

Truth be told, I probably only understood about half of the plan, and even then I was sketchy on some of the finer details. I wasn't in the least concerned, though. To me, the plan was merely a building block, a starting point from which I could go off-piste and improvise. Imagine, if you will, a jazz musician. Now imagine him improvising upon a detailed plan he had been given for the day of Kenneth's funeral by Mystery Man. I was that jazz musician.

I stood by the side of the road, ready to put Phase One into action. As had been outlined many times by Mystery Man, the lights turned red and the limousine stopped. It was then that I experienced a minor crisis of confidence. Was I supposed to go in the limo or stay where I was and let it drive away? I tried in vain to remember what Mystery Man had said about Phase One. A limo definitely figured into it somehow. Would be weird for him to mention it if I wasn't meant to get in. The lights turned to amber. Time to use my own initiative. The lights turned green, the limo started to move. Rushing forward, I opened the door, and with the sound of screeching tires in my ears and bebop playing in my heart, I jumped in.

If Hamish felt any surprise at me jumping uninvited into his limo then he certainly hid it well. There was perhaps a slight widening of the eyes and possibly a momentary nostril flare, but almost immediately these were displaced by his customary calm smile. 'Ah,' he said. 'Cudgel. Here you are. In the back of my limousine.' He reached out a hand for me to shake.

'We can do better than that,' I said, and pulled him tight for a bear hug.

'Yes,' said Hamish, disentangling himself, 'You were always a keen hugger.'

He opened a cupboard to his right and picked out a bottle of champagne. 'Tell me,' he said, reading the label, 'What brings you here, into the back of my moving car.'

'To be frank, it's all part of a complex plan-…' I began.

'Uh huh,' said Hamish, still focused on the bottle.

The thought occurred that he was not giving me his undivided attention. I considered Mystery Man's final words before we parted: 'For God's sake don't just blurt out the plan'. I needed to be more cunning. Vital to keep one's wits about one in such a high stakes game. Try to get some of the talking points in.

'So,' I said, playing it cool, 'Been hanging with any international criminals of late?'

'Would you like a glass of champagne?' said Hamish.

'Absolutely,' I said. Actually, I really didn't. Keeping a clear head was crucial. Plus, on the few occasions I had imbibed champagne I had been struck with the curious and overwhelming urge to sing as loudly as possible.

Hamish handed me a glass and raised his in toast. 'To Kenneth,' he said.

'To Kenneth.' I took a small sip. As I had feared, it tasted like golden liquefied happiness. 'Mmm, that's the good stuff right there,' I said, involuntarily shuddering. I took a bigger sip.

'Oh, the Grand Old Duke of-…'

'I wonder about poor Kenneth,' said Hamish, shaking his head sadly. 'What kind of man winds up getting stabbed in the back? A terrible way to go. And what kind of man stabs another man in the back? Why would one man do that to another man? And, more pertinently, *who* would do that to another man? *Who*, I wonder? Who would do that? Who do you think would do a thing like that?'

He stared at me with an odd intensity. It was like he was asking me a question. I took a long swig of champagne and held out my glass for a refill.

'Professor Pargus, maybe?' I said.

Abruptly Hamish's face changed to look of confusion. '*Really*?' he said, filling up my glass. 'Our old university Professor? The celebrated author and noted thinker? Why would you think he would have a major role to play in Kenneth's terrible, terrible murder?'

86

I took a pensive sip, also feeling confused. Fair enough, Professor Pargus being a master criminal wasn't exactly public knowledge, but from what Mystery Man and Sally had told me, Hamish was pretty much his go-to guy. Hmm. Hmm squared. There seemed to a small chance, unlikely and implausible as it seemed, that Hamish was trying to trick me somehow.

'Tell me,' said Hamish, leaning in closer and smiling broadly, 'What do you know about the Professor? Tell your old friend Hamish. Who told you to come into this limousine? Tell me.'

Lying is not my nature, especially to my old friend Hamish. The need to tell him everything was suddenly compelling. This was the pickle's pickle indeed. I took another swig of champagne to buy some time and to again experience a taste that at once seemed to confirm the existence of God yet challenge His authority. As I swallowed the car stopped at a red light, the jolt causing me to spit out my champagne. It went all over Hamish.

'No matter,' he said, grimacing slightly. 'Where were we?'

'Sorry,' I coughed. I coughed again. That was it! I coughed once more. And again. Soon I was in the middle of a full blown coughing fit.

Hamish's smile stretched to breaking point as he waited for me to stop. But that I had no intention of doing. On and on I coughed. With grace and majesty I coughed. For Kenneth and for Mystery Man I coughed. Most of all I coughed for myself. Hamish would not trick me with his sparkling words and awe-inspiring champagne. For I had coughing on my side.

After roughly eight minutes, Hamish finally snapped. 'What the hell is wrong with you?' he screamed. Upon these words the limo stopped. There was a burst of static from the intercom.

'We're at the church,' said the driver.

Quickly downing the last of the champagne, I swung open the door and burst out of the limo.

'Thanks for the lift!' I called back to Hamish. Rare was the occasion I had felt this much pride in myself. Skipping into the church, grin on face, I doubted there was a happier man in the entire funeral congregation.

The place was packed. Finding a seat would be tricky. Hamish swept passed me, giving me the sort of subtle smile a layman might mistake for a scowl. He moved up to the pews at the front and took a seat beside Sally and Donald. My heart swelled as I saw the Sally was still wearing my trousers, her face still coated with her own blood.

Instead of his wife, the space beside Donald was occupied by a set of crutches. I supposed that Susan must not have been strong enough to support Donald in the same way a good set of crutches would, but it still seemed a shame for her to miss out on all the fun. These, I imagined, were the tough calls and hard decisions that make up a marriage.

Hamish reached Donald and Sally. From forty feet away, across a crowded church, I was unable to hear what he was saying, even when cupping my hand to my ear and leaning forward. Vaguely recalling part of the plan where Mystery Man said I should hang back at the funeral, I didn't join them up front. Also, I was feeling a little guilty about not just telling Hamish everything in the back of the limo. Best to give him some time to cool off. Hopefully by the end of the funeral he would be over it. I reckoned he would. He was a laid-back cat who was never the type to remember slights and hold grudges.

Looking around at the assembled mourners, it became apparent that Kenneth had known a lot of people that I personally did not know. It was like he had an entire life outside of the confines of our friendship. This epiphany made me unsteady on my feet and I grabbed hold of the nearest chair. It was sturdy, yet coated in a soft black material identical to my jacket. I stroked it a little. It wasn't made of wood, but it wasn't cushioned either. I concluded that it was in fact not a chair but someone's shoulder. This was confirmed when the owner of said shoulder stood up to face me.

'What?' he said.

I once read someone describe coincidences as the purest form of magic. The argument went that the greatest work of illusionists and conjurers paled into insignificance compared to the random glorious magic of chance. Now, clearly the proponent of this gambit must never have seen a magician's assistant being sawn in half whilst immersed in a hundred gallons of water while wearing a straightjacket, but standing there in the church I was inclined to take their point. For whose shoulder should I have grabbed but the large fellow from the café.

'It's you!' I said.

The large fellow certainly recognised me. It was clear from the look on his face and suddenly downcast eyes. Why was he being so shy? Without another word he turned and sat back down. Maybe it was because I hadn't chatted to him yesterday. Still, there was plenty of time to make up for that. I had found someone I knew at the funeral and I'd be damned if we weren't going to have several minutes of pleasant small talk before the festivities began.

'Been back to the café?' I asked, sitting down beside him.

'Dunno what you mean,' said the large fellow. He stared intently at his knuckles, which to be fair were covered in some interesting tattoos.

'Yesterday at the café? You kept staring at me, then I looked up and you went back to reading your newspaper?'

'Dunno,' said the large fellow again, continuing to gaze knuckle-wards. I impressively contorted my body so my head lay on top of said knuckles, and our eyes finally met.

'Hello!' I said, looking up at his large head, framed from my vantage point by the stained glass windows. It was an oddly beautiful image.

'Get off!' said the large fellow. Not realising that his body was supporting my weight, he chose this moment to stand up. Naturally, I fell. Fortunately, the knee rest was pulled down and my landing was gentle. Lying there was actually quite comfortable and had it not been for my desire to properly befriend the large fellow I may have very well stayed there for the entire funeral.

The large fellow, with his trademark inscrutability, was presently making his way to the other side of the church. Bound by the velvet handcuffs of friendship, I was obliged to follow. Once more, I placed a hand on his shoulder. 'Me again!' I said.

'Stop following me,' said the large fellow.

'Stop moving then!' I said jovially. 'What shall we chat about?'

'I can't talk to you.'

'Why's that?'

'Professor Pargus said I'd not to.'

See what I mean about coincidences! The large fellow also knew Professor Pargus. This really was the truest of magic. I was keen to let him know that we shared a mutual friend, but as I was about to do so, the organist started to play a slow, sad tune. The funeral had begun.

'We'll chat after,' I assured the large fellow.

The service was a bit dull. Prayers were murmured and hymns sung. I know there's a procedure to these things, but for a one-off like Kenneth I felt they could have jazzed it up a bit. Father Carlo did his best, but you can only work with the material you're given. Nevertheless, I kept my feelings under wraps and chose not to boo at any stage, limiting myself to a slow hand-clap during the offertory.

After what seemed like an age, things finally started to get going. Father Carlo announced that those closest to Kenneth would now be saying a few words. Though it was a touch cheeky of him to throw this on me with no prior warning, I of course had no

shortage of anecdotes and tributes to relay.

I slipped out of my chair and towards the altar, noticing that Donald seemed to be heading in the same direction. He had a good forty feet head start on me, but with the fairly serious damage that had been inflicted on his legs, I didn't doubt that I could beat him up there. But, feeling a slight guilt about my small role in his injuries, I magnanimously slowed down.

After a really long time, Donald reached the altar. He grasped both hands to the lectern and stared at the microphone in front of him. A dramatic pause. Yes, that was an excellent way to start a speech. Finally he looked up towards the congregation.

'This…' he began, '…this is a microphone.' No one could deny the accuracy of this statement. All told, a strong start. He reached into his pocket and pulled from it a bottle of vodka – a masterstroke. Donald took a long swig from the bottle, and then placed it down lovingly on the lectern. He drew his face closer to the microphone and belched.

'Ahm…pardon me. I'm here today to talk about a friend of mine. Kenneth. Recently was alive, now isn't. Stabbed in the back. Who would kill him? Why would he be killed? How should I know?'

Then the speech took a bit of a left turn. 'But what can I say? I'd known the man for years and I can't say I liked him. Bit of a smug arse. Always so happy. Happiness. *Happiness*. Let me tell you about happiness. There's no such thing! Are you here, Susan? No, of course not. But I know all about you and Alfonso! Oh yes, I know all.'

Donald grabbed his crutches and moved purposefully from the altar. Sadly, his determination outstripped his physical capabilities and he crashed down the steps and onto the floor. He proceeded to grab the hat of an elderly lady in the front row and vomit into it with great gusto. Returning it to its owner he slowly resumed his seat.

Feeling unsure to top this performance, I edged my way up the aisles. But yet again, I was beaten to the punch, this time by Sally. Had it been anyone else, I would have considered removing them by force and taking my rightful place centre stage. Seeing as it was Sally, though, I contented myself to mouthing 'I love you', and giving her a coy little wave.

'I knew Kenneth for a long time,' she began. 'I am sorry he ended up getting stabbed. It is a tragedy. Yet part of me feels he must have in some way wanted it to happen. For Kenneth to be stabbed is a shock, yet whoever he angered must have had a good reason to do it. If I were to give one message to the person that stabbed Kenneth, it would be, "I'm on your side". Kenneth's death is a tragedy, and not something I would want to happen to me. Thanks everyone.'

With that Sally walked down the aisle, straight past me and out of the church. A performance like that fully merited the standing ovation it received. I whooped and cheered, slightly confused that no one else was joining in.

Finally, *finally* it was my turn to speak. Time to say what was on my mind and get some thoughts off my chest. Yes, about Kenneth but also some more generalised musings. Though I didn't have anything prepared I knew the stage was set for an epic on par with the Gettysburg Address, only not fictional. I was nearly at the altar before realising that Hamish had beaten me to it.

Despite the myriad wonderful thoughts I knew I could impart, it seemed right, what with our recent bad blood, to let Hamish speak first. I took his seat in the front row and gave him my rapt attention.

'Thank you all for coming,' he said. 'I'm sure Kenneth would have appreciated it. And thank you to Donald and Sally for their contributions. Individuals to a fault. I think about Kenneth, and I think about how he is now dead, and what a tragedy that is.

But I'm also sure that if Kenneth were here now and not dead, he'd

want all of us to move on. We must look to the future and not dwell

on the hows and the whys and the whos. He was stabbed, and that's

that. Yet even as I say this, I realise that if one lesson can be taken

from Kenneth's death, it's that anyone can be stabbed at any time,

so don't mess with things that don't concern you.'

At this crucial moment in the speech, Hamish, thrillingly

chose to look directly at me. 'I hope I've made myself clear,' he

said, then left the altar and sat down beside me.

'Great speech,' I whispered to him.

He frowned and whispered back, 'Were you not paying

attention?'

'Of course, you spoke beautifully. Right my turn.'

No one could stop me now. I jumped up to the lectern and

grinned at the crowd. Clearing my throat, I was as interested as

anyone to find out what my first sentence would be. Out of

nowhere, the organist started playing and in an instant the whole church was singing again and before I knew it, the place was emptying and it was clear that I wouldn't be getting the chance to speak after all.

I stood sadly, feeling pretty sorry for myself. Quickly, I snapped out of it. Mystery Man was relying on me. The next stage of the plan was to take place at the reception at Kenneth's house. But how to get there? Despite my praise for his speech, it was unlikely Hamish would give me a lift. Sally had already left and Donald was probably in no state to drive. It was a tricky situation. Then, shining out of the crowd like a big beautiful bald beacon, I saw the large fellow nearing the exit. Knowing I would have to be quick, I kicked the lectern aside and raced through the throng, pushing aside mourners old and young.

Not wanting to break our tradition, I placed my hand on his shoulder. 'Me again!' I said. 'I've got a favour to ask.'

'Can't help you,' he said, with his trademark reserve.

100

'I need a lift to Kenneth's house. I assume that's where you're off to?'

The large fellow looked more tongue tied than ever. Poor man, he really wasn't the sharpest. 'You need to quit bothering me,' he said. 'Professor Pargus will be angry.'

It was time to allay his fears. 'Look,' I said kindly, 'I know Professor Pargus. We're very close. I'm very interested in finding out what he's got up his sleeve. So meeting you here, right now, is a blessing. Come on, friend. Let's go to Kenneth's.'

Despite how clear I was being, the large fellow still looked confused. 'What's your game?' he said.

Patience is one of my strongest virtues. Top five anyway (humility is number one, by a distance). Sometimes though, people can just be so silly. I sighed, thinking how I could just kick the large fellow in the kneecap then follow up with a quick uppercut to the jaw. The big silly billy. 'There's no *game*. We're friends and I'm asking you for a favour. Unless you consider what Mystery

101

Man and I are doing to be a game. Personally, I view it more as a plot. Or a scheme.'

Still, the large fellow stood there, looking as confused and bald as a baby that's just woken up. 'No,' he said finally and walked away.

I hadn't wanted it to come to this, but again I was in a situation where violence was the only logical recourse. Feeling the familiar heady mix of adrenaline and excitement in my bones, I zeroed in on the large fellow's kneecap.

Before I had the chance to kick, his phone rang. My foot dropped back to the ground. Never polite to kneecap someone when they're on the phone. Eavesdropping on his call was an unfortunate but necessary evil. Difficult to get a proper sense of a conversation when only hearing one side, though.

'Hello,' began the large fellow, which could have meant anything.

'Uh huh,' he said. Then, 'Yes.' He turned to look at me and followed up with an 'Are you sure?' before closing on a 'Yes sir'.

All in all fairly inscrutable. If forced to hazard a guess, I would have wagered he had been on the phone to his mother, perhaps in relation to coming round for lunch at the weekend. It was just an intuition, but it felt right.

'How's your mum?' I said.

'What?' said the large fellow.

Honestly, had he not *just been on the phone to her*? One could argue he deserved a kick then and there for being so stupid, but that's probably politically incorrect in the current climate.

'Fine,' said the large fellow. 'I'll give you a lift to Kenneth's house.'

'Yay!' I said.

It was a frosty journey. The large fellow took what I considered to be an incredibly convoluted route to Kenneth's, intent on following signs and clearly defined roads rather than taking any of the shortcuts I suggested. Initially I limited myself to yelling, 'No, *left*, you moron!' or similar tips. After a fashion though, it was clear that the only thing for it was to take matter into my own hands, in this instance literally. I leaned over and grabbed control of the wheel.

'What are you doing?' said the large fellow in alarm, as if this wasn't the logical endgame of his incompetence.

'I'm *trying* to get us to Kenneth's house,' I said stemming his attempts to push me off by elbowing his nose.

The car swerved on the road, first to the right, then the left, then really *really* to the left, then a little to the right, then back to our original position, then a little more left.

'Quite the rollercoaster!' I said, as one of the wing mirrors was scythed off by a passing lorry.

'Okay, okay, I'll let you drive!' said the large fellow.

I looked at him, confused. 'I don't know how to drive,' I said, giving the wheel a sharp tug rightwards. We were at

Kenneth's house. Spotting Mystery Man hiding behind a nearby bush, beckoning me over, I turned to the large fellow, who was already making his way to the front door. 'Thanks for the lift, large fellow,' I said. 'Fun times.'

I hurried over to Mystery Man. 'We don't have much time,' he said. Undeniably true. In the great scheme of things, we're not on this planet for very long. Life passes so quickly and you must make every moment count. Standing there, on that day, outside the memorial reception of a close friend, hiding behind a bush, those words rang truer than ever. How apt, how quintessentially Mystery Man it was to have said those words at this time.

'God, you really nailed it there,' I said.

'What? In fact, never mind. We're close here. Remember the plan. Get Sally, Donald and Hamish together in Kenneth's bedroom. Get them talking about Kenneth. Then, I'll have Pargus. Is everything clear?'

'Yes,' I nodded, then realised I was telling the truth. It was a simple plan and it played to my strengths. I loved getting the gang together and I loved talking about Kenneth. How marvellous that these hobbies could be used to take down an international criminal. I continued nodding at Mystery Man.

'Stop nodding,' said Mystery Man. I obliged and a period of silence followed. Without Mystery Man relaying the plan or me nodding we were just two guys hiding out in a bush.

'So...now you go inside and enact the plan,' said Mystery Man.

'Right!' I said, springing from the bush and brushing the twigs from my hair. I straightened my tie and cracked my knuckles, slapped my face and bit my tongue. The front door loomed in front of me. I stepped inside the house.

*

My immediate thought was that the house was extremely big. I knew Kenneth had been no pauper, but never could I have envisaged an interior so spacious. Open mouthed I wandered down the high-ceilinged hallway, marvelling at the beautiful paintings as well as the excellent shade of green Kenneth had painted the walls.

The living room was huge. In another time it might have been a ballroom, or perhaps a paddock for house trained horses. Seats and couches lined each of the walls, save for one which was given over to a long buffet table. The place was packed, and gloom flavoured whispers snaked through the sea of black clothes. Frankly, it was a total downer and I resolved to find Sally, Donald and Hamish as soon as possible.

Hard to remain incognito on a scavenger hunt, though. Needed to play it cool, keep it casual. I was just a regular guy, having a regular time at his close friend's wake. Casually, I climbed on top of a chair to get a better look at the room. Nothing.

Nothing but a range of unfamiliar haircuts of varying lengths and consistency.

All I could do was wait. Idly, I pulled some books from the bookcase in the vain hope it might spin around to reveal a secret chamber. Picking one of them up, I sat on a couch.

When there's time to kill, nothing beats a good sturdy book. Carefully, I tore out page one. Plenty of opportunities to perfect making a paper aeroplane.

At page eighteen I noticed that someone was standing directly in front of me. Reaching page thirty one, it seemed polite to look up and see who it was.

'Hello Cudgel,' said Sam.

'I'm trying to make a paper aeroplane. It's not going very well.' I gestured to the growing pile of crumpled rubble beside me. 'It's hard not to blame the paper.'

'Give me a go,' said Sam, sitting beside me. She took the book, ripped out page 142 and set to work. With her small hands working furiously she resembled a squirrel I'd seen gathering nuts in the park some years ago. I mentioned this to her.

'Mmm,' she said, tearing out more pages, 'I've been told I have a squirrel-like aspect.'

She seemed consumed by her work, oblivious to my shouts of encouragement. So, I contented myself with watching her. Like Sally, she was a woman. Like Sally she also had hair and eyes and clothes and teeth and shoes. Yet in spite of these shared characteristics they were quite different. Where Sally was tall and boisterous, Sam was quiet and quite small. While Sally favoured the patterned and colourful, Sam was wearing a black jacket with a black shirt, black trousers and heavy looking black boots. Sally's hair was long and dark and flowing, instantly redolent of stolen summer nights years ago, the smell of strawberries in the air as she danced at the Graduation Ball. Sam's hair was short and bleached white and reminded me of nothing so much as Male Sam.

'Where is Male Sam, by the way?' I asked.

Sam stopped and looked at me, and her eyes momentarily shone like two conkers in the rain. 'Probably with Sally,' she said.

She continued to gaze at me. It appeared I was expected to say something. But what? What could possibly be wrong with him being with Sally? Sally was great. I wished I was with Sally.

'Is that...' I struggled to think of the right words, '...not wonderful?'

Without removing her eyes from mine, Sam stamped on my foot. Her boots were indeed heavy.

'Ow!' I remarked.

'They're welcome to one another,' she said, standing up.

'Here,' she placed the book on my lap. On top of it lay a perfect paper aeroplane, with a squadron of smaller planes around it. In addition were two tiny paper people replete with paper parachutes.

I gazed up in awe. 'Magnificent!' I said.

She cocked her head to the side and gave me look like a cat weighing up the feasibility of jumping from one wall to another. She sat back down.

'So what are you doing here?' she asked.

I looked down at the parachute people. Anyone who could fashion them had to be trustworthy.

Starting from the very beginning, and leaving nothing out, I told her the whole saga thus far, from discovering Kenneth with the knife in his back to sitting on the couch at his wake. Sam seemed surprisingly unperturbed.

'I knew about Professor Pargus,' she said. 'I've met him quite a few times. And when Sally gets drunk she loves to brag about her criminal days. Also when you at were at the flat the other day I was in the room when Sally told you all that stuff. Remember?'

'Do you think she might have killed Kenneth?'

111

'No, I don't think so. If she did we would have taken pictures of it for one of her projects. Plus, she's worried Professor Pargus is going to get her next.'

'Ah,' I said, as Sally's speech at the funeral started to make sense. 'Did I mention the large fellow?'

'Several times. His name is Alan. He works for Professor Pargus. He used to do work for Sally too sometimes. Bodyguard stuff, lifting things. She once painted his entire body red.'

Alan. Yes, that was a good name for the large fellow. I swirled it around my mouth, tasting its short, blunted corners.

'Oh,' I said, 'I haven't even told you about the plan Mystery Man gave me.'

Almost as soon as I said his name, Mystery Man materialised from the mourners and made a bee-line to Sam and me.

'Just in time,' I said, 'I was about to start relaying the plan.'

Over the course of our friendship, I'd estimate that Mystery Man's face had expressed some level of anger around 70% of the time. Enough to suggest that it was probably his default demeanour. However, at my greeting, he reached a level I hadn't seen before. His face was so red I wondered if Sally had painted him à la Alan. When he finally spoke, it was in a hoarse whisper. 'Why are you telling her the plan?'

It seemed necessary to relax him. 'Don't worry,' I said. 'This isn't just some nobody. This is Sam. She's very close to Sally.'

'*Was* very close to Sally,' said Sam.

'What do you mean?' I said.

'Do you realise what you've done?' said Mystery Man, but I paid no heed.

'What do you mean?' I said again to Sam.

'I've left Sally and Sam to each other. Sally especially, I can't deal with her anymore.'

'You…hate Sally?' I said.

'*Years* of work…' continued Mystery Man.

'I don't like the word hate,' said Sam. 'But sometimes I guess it's appropriate.'

Abruptly, I stood up and threw the book down on the couch, crushing the large plane, the small plane and the two tiny parachutists. 'Good day to you both,' I said, as Mystery Man began screaming into a cushion.

'Wait, where are you going?' said Sam.

I didn't answer. In a daze, I stumbled across the room, bumping into chairs and people alike. Sitting down at the buffet table I quietly wept. She hated Sally. *Hated.* The last few days had certainly held some revelations, but this was too much. Seeking comfort, I began nibbling on the hors d'oeuvres. On the other side of the room, through the crowd, Mystery Man and Sam were deep in conversation. This was odd. What in God's name were they talking about? Perhaps they had a mutual friend. Maybe they

114

supported the same football team. Maybe. Even after my second

plate of (fantastic) sautéed mushrooms they had not let up.

Arguably the thing to do was to swallow my feelings and go

and ask them something along the lines of, 'What are you two

talking about?' Yet I had stormed away and the key rule about

storming away is that one must never storm back, no matter if the

storm has retreated into a petulant drizzle.

At a loss, I searched for some more mushrooms. Then I

searched my soul. A case could be made that it would be wrong to

leave Mystery Man with a confirmed Sally-hater like Sam, lest she

be attempting to poison his mind. Then again, if I was being

honest, Mystery Man had never expressed any great fondness for

Sally. In fact, there had been times when he'd gone as far as to

criticise her art work. Despite this, I loved Mystery Man with all

my heart. With Kenneth dead he was one of several vying for the

coveted position of my official best friend. What then, was my problem with Sam? Why was I reacting like this? Normally, I didn't even like mushrooms.

Sometimes in life one has to admit they don't know the answer to a question. To unpick the intricacies of my brain I would need the help of a skilled psychiatrist. Anxiously, I scanned the room to see if there were any kicking about.

An elderly man stopped by the buffet table. He had grey hair and an impressive skull shape. I sat him down beside me. 'What is my problem with Sam?' I asked.

The psychiatrist looked at me solemnly. 'Did you eat all of the mushrooms?' he said.

A riddle. Naturally. But seeing through his mind games and psycho-babble I understood what he was trying to say. Yes, of course I had eaten all of the mushrooms, and yes, *of course* I should let bygones be bygones with Sam and re-join her and Mystery Man on the couch. It was all so simple. I patted the psychiatrist on his big clever head. 'You've helped me with a lot of my issues. You're a good egg.'

I marched back over to the couch, pushing aside furniture and people. I was back where I belonged, at the couch with Mystery Man and Sam and all was right with the world. 'I ate all of the mushrooms,' I announced. 'But the large-skulled psychiatrist made me understand that it was okay. I understand now. I understand it all. We shook hands and I marched triumphantly.' I paused for breath. Sam gave me an understanding nod. 'And I'm sorry,' I added, a touch unnecessarily.

'Right,' said Mystery Man. 'If you're finished, Sam here is going to help us. We've been talking. Normally I wouldn't change a plan this late on, but desperate times...' he gestured at me. I waved back.

Glad as I was that Mystery Man had taken my suggestion on board and decided to include Sam in the fun, it all meant nothing if the major players weren't in the living room. 'How am I meant to get Sally, Donald and Hamish together in the same room if none of them are here?' I turned to Mystery Man in askance to be confronted by the sight of him no longer being there.

'He left a few seconds ago,' explained Sam. 'You weren't paying attention.'

'Oh,' I said.

Sam elbowed my ribcage. 'Donald just walked in,' she said.

'Walked' wasn't quite the right term to describe Donald's method of movement. 'Staggered' is a little closer, but still not perfect. His old knee injury, mixed with the beating I'd been forced to give him in the clubhouse, along with his fall from the altar earlier, had clearly all caught up with him. Added to this was the unmistakable sense that he'd been drinking a fairly substantial amount of alcohol, as evidenced by the near empty bottle of whisky he held jealously to his chest. It was a testament to his physical strength and mental toughness that he was standing at all. A lesser man would have collapsed crying long ago.

Donald collapsed onto the couch, crying. Sam and I exchanged a brief glance that was enough to concoct a plan. I dove onto Donald and gave him a bear hug.

'No, don't do that!' Sam was apparently liable to change her mind on plans with no notice.

'I'm so sorry, Mr Danworthy,' she said, pulling me off Donald with surprising strength for a small person.

'Aaargh,' added Donald.

Okay, we'd do things her way. At least I'd be there to pick up the pieces if it failed. Donald saw me sitting beside him on the couch and covered his legs. Did he think I was going to attack him again? How odd.

'I must say, Mr Danworthy, I've always been a big fan of yours.' Sam pushed me out the way and took up the spot beside Donald.

'Is...is that so?' A roguish smile began to break out on his face, closely followed by a loud and hearty belch.

'At art school, I had a picture of you on my wall. I don't even like golf.'

'But *he's* a golfer,' I tried to explain. Sam stamped on my foot.

'Is that so?' Donald leaned closer to her, swaying slightly.

'That is so.' Sam leaned closer to him. All told they were leaning very close to each other. It was hard not to feel left out.

'How about...' said Sam, stretching the last syllable well outside of its comfort zone, '...we go somewhere and you explain golf to me?'

Donald made a grunting noise, like a bull goring a matador, or maybe a matador being gored by a bull.

'Let's say the main bedroom in fifteen minutes?' said Sam.

'I'll be there,' grunted Donald.

'So will I.'

'Me too!' I said, earning myself another stamp on the foot.

Sam slowly got up from the couch, smirked at Donald and headed towards the buffet table.

'Didn't expect that to work,' I said. Noticing me again, Donald saw fit to grab the whisky bottle and start swinging. It seemed a good a time as any to leave the couch.

'Well, that's one down,' said Sam at the buffet table, her mouth full of stuffed pepper.

'Good thing you were such a fan of Donald at art school,' I said. Sam found this remark monumentally funny. She had a loud laugh, like someone banging their head off a car horn. Abruptly she stopped, her eyes narrowing. Following their beady trajectory I found myself staring at Sally.

She had chosen to enter via the medium of Male Sam giving her a piggy back. Together they bounded round the room, Sally giggling and shouting, 'Faster!' as her legs swung wildly. My psychiatrist friend happened to be in the wrong place at the wrong time, receiving a boot to the face and landing headfirst in a plate of mushrooms. I made a mental note to remark on this cruel irony at our next session.

The psychiatrist slowly got to his feet and wiped his face clean of the delectable fungi. Straightening his suit and running a hand through his magnificent hair, he approached Sally and Male Sam, who stood proudly in the centre of the room as everybody else moved fearfully to the walls.

'Excuse me,' said the psychiatrist.

'What?' Sally stopped giggling.

'You're being extremely disruptive and rude'.

'Are we?' said Sally. 'How…*wonderful*. Spin, Sam. Spin!'

On this command, Male Sam began spinning round.

'Now really!' said the psychiatrist, raising his voice for the first time, perhaps ever. 'That is quite enou-…'

Sadly, we were unable to find out how the psychiatrist had intended to finish this sentence, as yet again he was caught hard on the chin by Sally's flailing foot. He stumbled slightly before falling with a not-insubstantial noise at my feet.

The room, which hitherto had been humming with minor key discontent, erupted in a chorus of anger. Riding in on the back of Male Sam was clearly one thing, nearly decapitating an elderly man another. It's funny where people draw lines in the sand.

As ever, amid the noise and recriminations, Sally's voice was the loudest. 'Oh shut up, all of you.' This had the remarkable effect of shutting everyone up.

The psychiatrist groaned and slowly got to his feet.

'Don't worry, old friend,' I consoled him. 'There's plenty more mushrooms over there.'

He groaned again in thanks and shuffled off, his movement causing Sally to look in our direction. Our eyes met. We held eye contact. I blinked. When I opened my eyes she was looking at Sam. I blinked again, then several more times. I scrunched my eyes tight then opened them as wide as they would go. No, she was still looking at Sam.

'Everyone go back about their business,' she shouted to the room. Just like that, the room went back about their business. Sally had one of those voices. 'There you are,' she said to Sam. Sam said nothing in return, choosing instead to stare at the floor and scowl.

'I think we've had all the fun we're going to have here today,' said Sally. 'But now I think it's best to go somewhere far away for a while. I'm thinking Morocco.'

'No,' said Sam, still staring with great interest at the ground. 'I'm not coming. I'm done.'

'Done?' said Sally.

'With the group. With everything,' said Sam, finally managing to turn away from the admittedly fascinating carpet and look Sally in the eye.

124

Sally looked confused, then extremely angry, before settling on sardonic. 'Is that so?' she said.

'If you want to discuss it, I'll be in the main bedroom upstairs in ten minutes. Come alone,' said Sam, looking pointedly at Male Sam, who had begun chewing dully on a carrot.

A pause followed. Sally seemed lost for words, an event so rare that everyone was too lost for words to fill the vacuum. 'Very well,' she said finally. 'Very well.'

'Oooh,' I turned to Sam. 'I see what you're doing. Yes, very good. Keep going.'

Sally looked at me. God help me, I wasn't going to blink. 'You're also here,' she said.

'Yes,' I replied, bashfully.

Sally clicked Male Sam with her heels. 'Move,' she said, and together they left us.

'That's that then,' said Sam, watching them go.

I must say, I was heavily impressed by Sam's ability to keep her eye firmly on the ball. Mystery Man really ought to have considered employing her earlier. Although, had that been the case I wouldn't have had the excellent experiences afforded to me over the last few days. That said, I was rather enjoying hanging out and working with Sam. We were a good team. I smiled at Sam. She stopped scowling and smiled back. Then I realised her smile extended over my shoulder and to the door, where Hamish had just entered.

'I feel I must be honest and forthright,' I said, as we watched Hamish glad-hand mourners.

'Okay,' said Sam.

'Okay,' I replied, and took a deep breath, holding it for a few seconds before exhaling. 'Okay,' I said again.

Sam folded her arms and tapped her feet, looking like someone who's been stopped by a faint acquaintance and can now see the bus they were waiting for recede into the distance.

I took another deep breath. 'Okay.'

'For God's sake what is it?' said Sam.

'Okay. Here's the thing. Hamish and I are great friends. Best friends. The best of friends. I love him. But today...' I took another deep breath, '...he's not in a very good mood with me.'

'Okay.'

'I can't be sure, but I think it's because I didn't tell him the plan earlier when he was asking. Maybe it's not that. But it could be. Yeah, I think it's that.'

'I understand.'

'Oh God, I feel terrible! I'm going to go and tell him the plan.'

I began to rush over to Hamish, but found my movement restricted as Sam grabbed my collar.

'You wait here,' she shoved me onto a chair. 'I'll talk to Hamish.'

Before I could reply, before I could regain circulation, she had gone. She was tough, no doubt about it. Rubbing my neck I watched as she talked to Hamish, hoping she had the presence of mind to apologise to him for me.

She returned with a satisfied look on her face. 'He's going up to the bedroom.'

'What did you say to him?'

Sam shrugged. 'I told him that Donald and Sally were meeting up there and that he should go and join them.'

'Ingenious.' I could never have come with a plan as intricate and cunning as telling the truth.

'So you better head up there then,' said Sam.

'What?'

'That's the next part of the plan, isn't it?'

Ah yes, so it was. The plan was really taking shape now. With a bit of luck the whole thing would be done in time for a late supper. I wondered if I had any cheese left in the house.

'Right. Off I go then.'

'Good luck.' Sam patted me on the arm, and then slipped into the crowd and out of the room before I had the chance to respond.

I hurried after her. We made such a good team I wondered if she wanted to accompany me on the final stretch.

'Found them!' said the psychiatrist, appearing before me with a smile on his face, a bag of ice against his head and a plate of mushrooms in his hand. Gently, I pushed him aside and made my way into the hall. No sign of Sam. No sign of anybody. The living room door closed behind me and suddenly all was quiet. This was it then. I took a moment to compose myself. It was time.

I looked up at the stairs before me. Tall, forbidding and undeniably stair-like. My legs felt both wobbly and leaden as I carefully placed a foot on the first step and began the climb. Actually, once I got going it was pretty much like climbing any other set of stairs and I reached the summit in around eight seconds. Then I was at the door to the main bedroom. This really *was* it. It really was *time*. As with the stairs though, opening it wasn't much of a challenge. I've opened plenty of doors.

And with that I had reached the promised land of the main bedroom. It would be difficult to argue that I had not carried out the plan in an exemplary manner. There were no surprises left in store. It was plain sailing from now on. Sighing happily I entered.

'What are *you* doing here?' said Kenneth.

*

As a youngster, I had been the proud owner of a hamster named Sean. Perhaps owner isn't the right term, for Sean was his own hamster and always acted as he saw fit. If that entailed subtly demanding more food through increased eye contact then so be it. If it meant biting me when he wasn't in the mood to hang then I had to accept it. Sean may have lived in a cage in my room but I could no more claim ownership of him than he of me. We were friends, we were equals.

Anyhow, after about six months Sean died. Following a weeklong grieving process I attempted to replace him with another hamster, named Morgan. But while Morgan shared many of Sean's characteristics and was undeniably also a hamster, there was something that didn't feel right. When Morgan died I moved onto Paula. Still a hamster, still acted like a hamster, still not Sean. After Paula there was Frank, then Ruth, then Leonard, Amber and Miguel.

Two things became clear. Firstly, hamsters don't live very long lives, at least not compared to the average human. Secondly, and more pertinently, it was time for me to admit that Sean was gone and no amount of replacement hamsters would change that. With death there is finality. With death there is no return.

All of which to say is that my immediate reaction to seeing Kenneth sitting on the bed was to scream, 'Impostor!' and attack him.

'Would…you…*stop*…attacking me,' said the impostor.

'I…can't…see…myself…stopping…anytime…soon,'   I replied, honestly.

There was more stifled conversation between us, but frankly, it all centred round the basic theme of the impostor not wanting to be attacked and me not being of a mind to stop. We continued in this vein for a good minute and a half, before I found my arms being pulled away. Then I was in a headlock and shortly afterwards pushed against the wall. Looking to see who had curtailed my assault I found myself staring at Mystery Man.

'Detective Arnold, can you *tell* this idiot what's going on, so he'll stop attacking me?' said the impostor.

I leaned close to Mystery Man's ear and whispered as quietly as I could. 'Try to be cool, but there's an impostor pretending to be Kenneth behind you.' Pausing, I tilted my head ever so slightly in the impostor's direction so Mystery Man would know who I was talking about. 'I think we should attack him together.' I gave Mystery Man a meaningful look. 'Also, who's Detective Arnold?'

'I told you to wait in the other bedroom,' said Mystery Man, letting go of me and addressing the impostor.

'It's *my* house. I'll wait where I want.'

'You've jeopardised the plan.' Mystery Man sat down beside him on the bed. 'Everyone will be here soon.'

I assumed Mystery Man was trying to ingratiate himself with the impostor before we sprung our double attack on him. However, he was definitely running the risk of inadvertently confusing me in the process.

'I'm feeling a little confused,' I said.

'I suppose you have every right to be.' Mystery Man stood up. 'But time is of the essence. Donald, Sally, and Hamish will be here any second.'

He looked at the impostor. 'We have to go under the bed.'

'*Such* an imposition,' said the impostor, but nevertheless followed Mystery Man's example by dropping to his knees and crawling under the bed. Good thing it was a king-size.

'To be totally upfront, Mystery Man, this has done nothing to ease my confusion,' I said.

'What the *hell* is he calling you?' said the impostor.

'There's a good explanation for everything,' said Mystery Man's voice from under the bed. 'But we're a bit pushed for time right now. The salient points are: yes, Kenneth is actually alive, and yes, I've known all along.'

'So what you're saying is that is actually Kenneth under the bed with you there?'

134

'*Yes*, you idiot,' said the apparently not-dead-after-all Kenneth.

I allowed myself a moment to take this in. 'I would very much like to jump up and down on the bed in happiness.'

'Obviously don't do that,' said Mystery Man. 'I'll explain everything later. Right now, it's vital you stick to the plan. When the three of them are here act like everything is normal. Do *not* tell them we're under the bed.'

This was tricky. Of course I wanted to aid Mystery Man with the plan. But here was my best friend, who I had last seen with a knife in his back, suddenly revealed to be alive and healthy without so much as a slight stoop. Everything I knew about humanity, truth and science had been ripped away from me. I had a lot of feelings.

'I'll…do my best.' I said, sitting on the bed.

'Don't *sit* on the bed, for God's sake.' said Mystery Man. I stayed seated.

With a jarring creak the bedroom door opened and Donald and Hamish entered.

'What are you doing here?' said Hamish.

I was a tense, sweaty mess. Inexorably, my eyes started inching themselves downwards, where a foot below, Kenneth and Mystery Man lay. *Under the bed*, I found myself mouthing.

'What the hell are you doing with your mouth?' said Donald. 'You better not come at me again. I'll take you out. And Hamish will back me up. Won't you, Hamish?'

'Hmm?' Hamish had been looking out of the window and then at his watch. The door opened and his eyes briefly flickered, only to darken again when he saw it was Sally. I smiled at her

'What are you doing here?' she said. She looked at Donald and Hamish. 'What are you *all* doing here?'

There was a momentary lull where it seemed like everyone was waiting for someone else to speak. I wondered when the last time all of the old gang had been in the same room together. Even with the small caveat of Kenneth hiding under the bed and everyone thinking he was dead it still felt wonderful.

'I was informed that that the two of you were to be meeting here. Thus here I am.' Hamish's eyes kept returning to the window. Maybe he was into bird-watching? That seemed like the kind of thing I'd know, though.

'Enough of the games, Hamish. Just tell us whether he's going to have us killed or not,' said Sally.

Hamish turned from the window and faced the room, his brow crinkled thoughtfully. 'I don't know what you mean,' he said.

'Don't play coy. We all know he trusts you the most. Tell me if I'm done for. Do you have any idea how much my art will be worth if I'm dead?'

137

Donald had been blowing his nose, a two-step process that involved extricating a tissue from his pocket followed by the act itself, both of which took a remarkably long time. His dedication to the task, not to mention the volume with which he performed it, had led him to miss Hamish and Sally's exchange. Only now, with the devastated tissue in pocket, did he deign to address the group. 'Clear off, eh. I'm meeting someone here.'

'I'm meeting Sam here, so you can clear off,' said Sally.

'Not a chance,' replied Donald, blowing his nose again, proving that a shirt sleeve is the equal of any tissue in that regard. 'She told me she wanted to meet me alone. That's right.'

Hamish's brow crinkled further. I can legitimately say I have never seen a brow so crinkled. 'So to be clear,' he said, 'This Sam person, in one way or another, has convinced all of us to come to this room at the same time?

'Looks that way,' I confirmed, thinking that I hadn't added anything to the conversation in a while.

'And you're here too, Cudgel,' said Hamish, his brow crinkled to such an extent it was in real danger of descending into self-parody.

Seemingly, these words caused Donald to remember I was in the room. 'Aargh!' he noted. 'Stay away!' He raised his crutch and swung it at me. Missing by a good four feet, in his unbalanced state he fell, landing eventually in my lap.

'There there.' I gently patted his head, which unfortunately he chose to view as a prelude to more violence. To stave off this imagined threat, he took the decision to get as far from me as possible. With his crutch on the other side of the room and his legs in less than perfect condition, his options were limited. In his golfing days, Donald had always been a dab hand at getting out of tricky situations. This ingenuity clearly hadn't left him and he concluded that his best and only recourse was to roll onto the floor.

He landed with a dull thud, followed by a bellow. 'What in bloody blue hell!'

It was quite likely he had spotted Kenneth and Mystery Man under the bed. Weighing up the options, it seemed best to pretend nothing untoward was happening. 'So, what's new with you guys?' I said.

'Kenneth's under the bloody bed!'

'Some weather eh?' I said.

'Kenneth's alive! He's under the bed with some other guy.'

'What is he talking about?' said Hamish.

I took a moment to gather my thoughts. 'Dunno,' I said.

'Okay, *okay*,' said Kenneth emerging from under the bed along with Mystery Man. Then the door to the room opened again and the large fellow entered, holding tightly a struggling Sam. Closely following them was none other than Professor Pargus himself, gun in hand.

It was hard to imagine a more action packed three seconds.

*

'Here we are then, the old gang back together.' Professor Pargus took in the room.

'Always nice to have a few more members on board, of course.' He pointed the gun in Mystery Man's direction.

I hadn't seen him in person for years. The vestiges of age were all too apparent. It was as if my memory of him had been put in the washing and come out wrinkled and faded. Still, he had an aura. In his trademark tartan suit he was a presence, a force. Now, as ever, the atmosphere, the *feel* of the room had irrevocably altered just by his stepping into it. The gun probably helped, admittedly.

'I thought the peyote might have worn off by now.' Sally looked at Kenneth, at Mystery Man, then the large fellow holding Sam. 'But maybe not.'

'Hello,' I said to Sam and the large fellow.

'Hello,' said Sam, elbowing the large fellow in the stomach.

'Stop *doing* that,' he said, annoyed.

'Ah, I think she means she wants you to let her go,' I deduced. The large fellow, as was his wont, ignored me.

'So, Detective Arnold, it's been a while eh? Been up to much? Any schemes on the go?' Professor Pargus wore the crooked grin he reserved for questioning the stupidest students in class. There was a song in his voice and his index finger beat a jaunty rhythm on the trigger.

Mystery Man said nothing. He seemed a little down. I think I understood why. Professor Pargus showing up hadn't been part of the plan. Everyone wants their plans to run smoothly, particularly when there's so much at stake. Also, having a gun in his face probably wasn't a barrel of laughs.

'I imagine,' said Professor Pargus, 'that the plan was to gather this lot together in a room, hope they would panic in light of Kenneth's "death", reveal my whereabouts and some incriminating details regarding my alleged criminalities. That about right? Tick all the boxes?'

'Spot on!' I replied, after it became clear that Mystery Man had no intention of joining the conversation.

For a moment I was the focus of the room. Professor Pargus's eyes were on me and I was reminded of the time in class I argued that T.S Eliot wrote terrible love songs. He turned back to Mystery Man. 'I have to say, I'm a little impressed. You've really gone the extra mile this time. Getting Kenneth here to fake his death. That takes a lot of doing. How did you keep that one from the rest of the force? You must have really wanted to get me. And to employ this idiot,' the Professor gestured towards me, 'you must have been *desperate*. One could almost feel sorry for you.' The Professor giggled, a surprisingly high pitched noise.

'Actually, this room's starting to feel a bit crowded. Sally, Donald, you may both leave.'

'Does that mean you aren't going to kill us?' said Sally

'What made you think I was going to do that?' said the Professor.

'I just thought, with Kenneth being kil-…Ah wait, never mind.'

'No, I wouldn't want you dead. Fearful certainly, but not dead. You should cite me more as an influence on your art, though. My work transcends form and genre.'

'Of course. Absolutely. Consider it done. Of course.' Sally hurried towards the door. She looked at Sam then at the Professor, who sighed.

'Very well. Always good to have a hostage but never mind. Let her go, Alan.'

The large fellow let go of Sam, who proceeded to give him an even harder elbow to the ribs, after which she followed Sally out of the room. Being honest, I was hoping for a goodbye or a 'Good luck with this interesting predicament' but neither was forthcoming. The door shut and she was gone.

'Good old Sally,' said the Professor. 'Can always rely on Sally. Unlike you,' he turned to Donald. 'What happened to you, eh? You used to be someone.'

Being in the Professor's presence had an odd effect on Donald. At first he seemed drunker and more dissolute. His head slumped and his lip trembled. Then, slowly, gradually, he drew himself up to his full height. His shoulders snapped back and if you were to squint you would say there was a brief moment where he resembled the Donald of his prime. 'Marriage,' he said.

The Professor clicked his tongue dismissively. 'That's no excuse. Now get out of here. I'm sure there's a bar waiting for you.'

Donald nodded, and with the aid of the large fellow, exited the room.

'See you soon!' I said, as they reached the door.

'Bloody better not,' said Donald.

Hamish, who had watched the proceedings like a particularly attentive cat, spoke. 'Sir, could I ask what the plan is? If you're to shoot everyone there will be quite the mess.'

'You know, I hadn't even thought that far ahead. I was still recounting Arnold's plan. Yes, I was saying the lengths he'd gone to, how much it had meant for him to get me. And for Kenneth to turn on me, go as far as to fake his own death. Detective, my hat is off to you.'

Professor Pargus looked at Kenneth. 'Anything to say for yourself?'

Kenneth hesitated, and then pulled out a gun from his jacket pocket.

The Professor's eyes grew comically large, his grin grew broader. I didn't have much experience with this kind of thing, but it seemed an odd reaction to someone revealing they were packing heat.

'Well then,' said the Professor. 'You guys have a gun, I have a gun. We have ourselves a good old fashioned stand-off.'

'Give up, Pargus,' said Mystery Man, drawing a gun from his own pocket. Lot of guns in the room now. It was an odd feeling, tense and taut like the second before you press a fire alarm.

With two guns pointed at him, Professor Pargus still seemed unperturbed. Maybe he was losing his mind. Maybe *Journey of the Space Ferret* was the first sign. Even Hamish was getting a bit concerned.

'Um, sir. I don't have a gun you know.'

'I know, Hamish, I would never trust you with a gun.'

'Right. Well, it's just there are three guns in the room and two are pointing at you.'

Professor Pargus nodded. 'I can see your point. Yet you must remember that I came from nothing to achieve great wealth and power. When I write I turn a blank page into gold. I am an alchemist, Hamish, I am a magician. And for my next trick...'

147

Professor Pargus clicked his fingers. Kenneth pointed his gun at Mystery Man.

'What are you doing?' said Mystery Man.

Professor Pargus let out a cackle. 'He's doing what he's always done – being loyal to me. Oh, Detective Arnold, to think you could ever turn one of my own against me.'

Mystery Man looked at Kenneth in fury. 'All this time, you were actually working for him?'

Kenneth laughed nervously. 'The Professor *thought* it would be funny.'

'The look on your face!' laughed Professor Pargus. 'Fantastic stuff. You really thought you had me.'

'The Professor thought I needed to *prove* myself after *Journey of-…*'

'We don't say that name,' hissed the Professor.

'So that's why I approached you,' said Kenneth. 'Sorry to have gotten your hopes up and all that.'

Mystery Man sat on the bed, looking crestfallen.

'Do I shoot him?' asked Kenneth.

'Don't be silly,' said the Professor. 'Taunting Arnold is the most fun I have these days. No, let him live to think he's going to catch me another day.'

'Sir, I really must interject!' said Hamish, louder than I can ever remember hearing him speak.

'What?'

'Well, sir. I knew nothing of this plan. You…you kept me out of the loop. I was dutifully trying to find out who killed Kenneth and waiting for you to arrive and now it turns out all of this has been happening the whole time.'

'What's your point, Hamish?'

'My point…my point is that you clearly don't trust me and after all I've done I would quite like to know why.'

The Professor shrugged. 'Just don't. Come on, Kenneth.' Without much ceremony, Kenneth and Professor Pargus left the room. The door shut and we could hear the sound of it being locked, which didn't seem the polite thing to do.

'Only the three of us left,' I said. It was hard to tell who looked more devastated between Mystery Man and Hamish. I sympathised - no one likes to feel as though they've been left out of a secret.

How to cheer them up? I considered both singing and dancing but it probably wasn't a big enough room to do it properly. Ventriloquism maybe? I had tried to learn the skill some years before but had given up when Monsieur Chuckles' insults grew too cutting. That only left card tricks, and given that I had never attempted to learn any and that there wasn't any packs of cards handy, I was in a tough spot.

But what if I were to do nothing at all? Might that help? Maybe the best thing to do was to let them both naturally emerge from their respective fugues. After which we could perhaps go for sandwiches. Yes, that sounded nice. Also, it had been a long day, a long week in fact, and a quick lie down definitely seemed in order.

Ignoring Mystery Man repeatedly slapping himself in the face and

Hamish's keening wails, I settled down on the bed and closed my

eyes, just for a second, just to relax.

*

I awoke some hours later to find Sam looking at me.

'I can't believe you fell asleep,' she said.

I looked around for Hamish and Mystery Man.

'Oh they're gone, it was a quite a to-do.'

It all returned to me; Kenneth being alive, Professor Pargus

coming in, a lot of guns, Kenneth turning on Mystery Man. So

much happening in such a short space of time. No wonder I had

needed a nap. Yet here, in the darkened aftermath, I began to feel

some regret. How stupid of me to have gone to sleep when seismic

events were clearly still taking place at regular intervals. Now here

I was in an empty room with only Sam for company. The sense that the narrative had moved on and that I was no longer a central part of things was overwhelming.

I sat up. 'So what happened here?' I said. Sam joined me on the bed, stretched her legs out, and began.

Upon being released by the large fellow and leaving the room, she had got into an argument with Sally. She was serious when she said that she did not wish to join her in Morocco. A fight had ensued, with Sam cheered on by the increasingly drunken mourners downstairs. After a hard fought draw, she bade an awkward farewell to Sally and Male Sam, who had phoned for a taxi somewhere around Round 2. She then downed some whisky to settle her nerves and happened to notice Professor Pargus and Kenneth sneaking out of the house. Quickly hiding so as not to have the imposition of being taken hostage for a second time in the same evening, she followed them outside where Alan, the large fellow, was waiting in the car for them, singing a slow sad song.

His singing voice was surprisingly beautiful, muscular yet subtle.

The three of them drove away and she took a moment to reflect that

it was odd for Kenneth to now be hanging out with Pargus since it

had seemed like he had gone to all the trouble of faking his death in

order for the Professor to be caught. Now incredibly curious to find

out what was going on in the bedroom she rushed back into the

house only to be accosted by a not-having-left-yet Donald, who

decided the time was right to get deeply, unsettlingly confessional

about his marriage. Not wanting to break him off mid-cry, yet also

feeling that time was somewhat of the essence, she had moved to

pat his shoulder, feigned falling over, kicked him in the shin and

ran upstairs. Reaching the bedroom door, she had discovered it was

locked and that inside a loud argument was going on between

Mystery Man and Hamish. From this, she gleaned that Kenneth had

been in league with the Professor all along. In the bedroom,

Mystery Man was imploring Hamish to tell him where Professor

Pargus's secret hideaway was. Hamish was reluctant, despite Mystery Man's undeniably valid point that the Professor clearly didn't trust or respect him and that Kenneth had proven to be definitively and forever the Professor's favourite. After some time, Hamish had cracked and it suddenly became emotionally very real. Hamish's fastidious need for order as a child and his absent father were among a number of subjects touched upon. Eventually, he explained where to find the Professor and after several attempts Mystery Man barged through the locked door. He was surprised to see Sam standing there. Having always loved a good adventure and with a surplus of time or her hands now she was free of Sally, taking down an international criminal seemed as good a way as any to spend an evening. She had pleaded with Mystery Man to let her help him all of the way down the stairs and out to his car. He was adamant in his refusal. This was his case and he was going to solve it alone, tonight. Other people can't be trusted. Keen as she was to go, there was a manic glint in Mystery Man's eyes that was slightly

154

discomfiting. He drove away and she decided to take another lap through the mourners and get some food. The sautéed mushrooms were indeed a revelation. At a loss at what to do next, she had gone up the stairs to the bedroom only to find Hamish was gone and that I had apparently been sleeping in the bed the whole time.

'And that's pretty much it,' she said.

'Excellent story,' I said. 'Really on point.'

Sam gave me a quizzical look. 'I can't believe you slept through all that shouting.'

'Yes, it is a little surprising. Then again, I've only slept once in the past week. And that was because I accidentally knocked myself unconscious.'

'Maybe that's it. So, what now?'

A good question. I was better for having napped, yet still felt I could perhaps do with another nine or ten hours sleep to be on the safe side. But with Sam relaying so much information to me it was vital that I took everything she had told me in. I lay back down

155

on the bed to really give myself some thinking space, pulling the covers over me so I would not be distracted by any outside noise, and closed my eyes to ensure I was fully committed to the task.

I woke several seconds later to Sam slapping my nose. 'Stop falling asleep.'

'I was ruminating on your words.'

'We need a plan.'

I nodded. '100%. Could not agree more. What about?'

Sam's palm thwacked my nostrils. 'About Professor Pargus. Detective Arnold knows where he is now. If he finds him I'm worried what Pargus will do.'

'Mystery Man is a warrior, a hero. It would take more than any one man to stop one man so great.'

'Professor Pargus has Alan as muscle too. And Kenneth, I suppose.'

'Oh yeah. Good thing Mystery Man doesn't know where Professor Pargus's secret hideaway is.'

'Hamish told him where it was. I literally just explained this to you.'

'Ah, I see…Yes…indeed...'

'Stop falling asleep!'

'Stop hitting my nose.'

Sam stood up and pulled the covers off the bed. 'Come on,' she said. 'We're going to save the day.'

I sighed, briefly fell back asleep, was awoken violently and then sighed again. 'How are we to save Mystery Man if we ourselves don't know where the secret hideaway is?' I asked, proud of my logic.

'I know where it is, I told you before remember?'

I stared at Sam blankly. 'When you went to Sally's building, we were in the close?'

It occurred to me that Sam might be losing her mind.

'Remember, I told you it was in Loch Tryg?'

Ah. *Ah.* 'I do remember!' I shouted proudly. 'Yes, you told me that, and I wasn't wearing any trousers. Yes, of course. Excellent.'

'So let's go there.'

'And save the day! Yes, let's go!'

With optimum effort, I extricated myself from the bed's smooth, pillowy embrace. In a matter of minutes I was on my feet, shoelaces tied, ready to leave the bedroom for the first time in quite some time.

'Shame I totally forgot you telling me about the hideaway,' I said, shutting the bedroom door behind us. 'Might have saved Mystery Man a bit of trouble. Ah well, all's well that ends well and all that.'

Together, we headed downstairs.

*

The night air was chilly and I wished I had thought to accessorise with an interesting scarf. Journeying from the bedroom had not been straightforward. The vast majority of the stairs had been negotiated easily, save for the last, occupied as it was by Donald and Hamish.

'Excuse us,' Sam had said politely.

'Excuse yourself,' said Hamish. I had never seen him in such a state. Normally so neatly put together, his tie was askew and his hair stuck out at a number of differing angles.

'He's had a bit too much to drink,' explained Donald.

With her slight frame, Sam was able to squeeze past without too much effort. With neither of a mind to move I was left with no recourse but to attempt to vault over them. I gave it my best effort and my jump was very nearly perfect save for my heel accidentally catching Donald on the jaw. After some time he regained consciousness and the ambulance crew arrived with admirable promptness. Anyway, it was probably about time Donald received some medical attention.

'Should we tell the mourners that Kenneth's not actually dead?' I asked Sam as we finally made it out of the front door.

She looked through the window to the living room, where the karaoke had begun in earnest. 'Let's not spoil their night.'

Presently, we were admiring the cars parked outside the house. 'Nice blue one there. Good shade of silver on that one. Sunroof too,' I said. Fun as this was I didn't see how it was going to get us any nearer to Professor Pargus's secret hideout.

'We're looking for a car to steal,' explained Sam. 'What did you think we were doing?'

'I thought we were just looking at cars.'

'I take it you've never stolen a car before?'

'I tried once. But I couldn't get through the lock. And it was a bike, not a car. And it belonged to me in the first place. Anyway, that's how I lost my bike.'

Sam stopped at small red convertible, roof handily down. 'This will do nicely.'

Hopping into the front seat like a black-clad kangaroo, she immediately set to work, her small hands whirring and whirling. Within seconds the engine started to clear its throat and soon began to roar. 'Let's go,' said Sam.

Despite Sam's advice to rest during the journey lest I 'fall asleep at some crucial moment and ruin everything', there was a question I needed answered; why, back in Sally's building had she told me where the secret hideout was?

Sam was quiet. Around us the city turned to green. The air grew colder still, stars suddenly visible. 'I needed a change,' she said eventually. 'I was done with Sally, and I could tell you were up to something. I don't know, in that moment helping you out just seemed like the thing to do.'

I nodded, pulling my jacket tight around me.

'Shall I put the roof up?' I heard Sam say as I closed my eyes.

I was awoken by her customary nose slap. 'We're here,' she whispered.

'Ouch,' I whispered back.

We had stopped at a clearing between two imposing sets of trees. Behind us was the main road, where the occasional car lit our faces and highlighted the darkness of the path in front of us. For the first time I began to regret surrendering my fantastic luminous trousers to Sally. Their combination of utilitarian function and aesthetic triumph really had been something to behold. I looked at my black suit trousers, blending perfectly into the surroundings and scowled. What was the point of going on a secret, covert mission if you couldn't even see your own trousers?

'Dark out here,' I noted. 'Lot of trees as well.'

'Yes,' agreed Sam. 'But stop talking so loudly.'

'Are we near the secret hideaway?'

'You think Professor Pargus would build his secret hideaway directly beside a main road?'

'It would be the last place one would think to look.'

Sam started heading up the path. 'We've got quite a walk ahead of us,' she said.

After twenty minutes of silent trudging in near darkness it was hard to shake the sensation that moaning about being cold and tired was absolutely the appropriate thing to do. The ground was soft and the fancy shoes Mystery Man had provided me with were undoubtedly getting filthy. It had started to rain and I could feel my shirt sticking unpleasantly to my stomach. Yet every time I opened my mouth to point any of this out to Sam she quickly admonished me. This was no time for talking apparently. Certain as I was that loudly whining about the situation would immediately improve it, I managed to restrain myself. I trusted Sam, and if she said to be quiet and walk through mud in the dark, then that was the way it had to be.

Imagine my surprise then, roughly an hour into our journey, when she stopped abruptly and spoke the first words between either of us in some time. 'Hmm.'

'Hmm?' I said.

'Yes. Hmm.'

'For what do you "Hmm"?'

'I think we might be lost.'

The massive trees leered nearly on top of us. In front of me, I could just about make out Sam scratching her head. 'Lost?'

'Lost.'

'As in don't know where we're going?'

'I know *where* we're going.' Faintly visible, she put her hands on her hips. 'I'm just not precisely sure how to get there.'

The night air seemed colder than ever. The darkness was taunting, a blanket covering who knows what. Trees took on ghoulish dimensions, a hiding place for ghosts, goblins and possibly even deer.

'I'm worried about the threat of deer.' I said.

'Deer won't hurt you, and they'll be asleep now.'

'That's what they'd have you believe.'

Sam took a few steps ahead, then to the left and right. 'I thought it was here,' she said. 'I was *sure* it was here.'

'How many times have you been?'

'Once. Six years ago. And we had all drunk one of Sally's special concoctions.'

'Was it fun?'

'Oh yes. There was a three hour spell where I was convinced I was a rabbit.'

That Sally had never thought to invite me to Professor Pargus's secret hideaway stung. Perhaps I had been busy that weekend.

'What shall we do now?' I said.

'I'm open to suggestions.'

Here was my chance. I had been happy following Sam and letting her dictate the game plan, but I must admit it felt good to be given a chance to put my own mark on things. The tricky part was to come up with a good idea; one that took into account our current predicament and our eventual goal. It was a difficult balancing act, but I knew within barely seconds that I had the perfect answer.

'We should shout as loud as we can for help.'

'That's a terrible idea,' said Sam.

'Help! Help! Somebody help us! We're lost and cold! Help! Help! Help!'

Sam punched me on the arm. 'Why did you do that? What if the Professor finds us?'

Aha. I hadn't thought of that. Undoubtedly, it was a fairly terminal flaw in the plan.

'We should get out of here.' Sam grabbed my arm and dragged me with her.

'Do you remember the way back?' I asked, panting as Sam broke into a jog, forcing me to keep pace.

'Not really, but better to get as far away as possible.'

This logic seemed sound and I concentrated on keeping up with her. Despite the conditions and the fact that her boots looked extremely heavy, she moved at a fair clip and soon I found myself struggling. Stitch in my side, panting like a panda in a sauna, I found myself slowing, Sam's grip loosening, before I fell to the muddy ground.

'For God's sake,' said Sam. 'We've only been running for a minute.'

'You…go ahead,' I wheezed, 'Leave me…here…to die.'

'Shut up,' said Sam.

'I…see…death,' I said.

'*Shut up*,' said Sam again. 'Do you hear that?'

Putting aside thoughts of my surely imminent demise, I listened. Listened intently. Listened with both ears.

167

'What am I listening for?' I asked.

'Someone's coming,' said Sam.

A flashlight in our eyes confirmed her suppositions.

'Halt! Halt, I say!' came a booming voice from the other side of the light.

'We've halted,' said Sam, shielding her eyes from the glare.

'Doubtful!' said the voice. 'I'll need some proof!'

'We've stopped walking. You've got a flashlight trained on us,' said Sam.

There was a pause after these words.

'You make a good point!' boomed the voice. 'I can't argue with any of that!'

With that he lowered the flashlight to the ground. The glare not so overwhelming, I was able to make out that our interrogator was a man of around fifty years of age. Even in the poor light, it was apparent that he had a moustache of magnificent and unwieldy proportions.

'You have both stopped! That much is now clear. But, now I must ascertain; what are you doing here?'

I stepped forward. 'First things first, let's talk about your moustache. I have several questions.'

Sam elbowed me.

'The first is a three parter.'

'Enough!' said our interrogator. 'I demand answers!'

Sam and I exchanged a look. I knew what she was thinking. Yes, it was imperative to get a clear answer about the moustache as soon as possible, but perhaps even more than this, it was vital that we not reveal our true purpose. One thing I had picked up from Kenneth double crossing Mystery Man was that Professor Pargus's reach was vast and all-encompassing. Strange as it sounded, there was a chance that this enigmatic and shadowy moustachioed man roaming around, apparently on the lookout for trespassers, was in fact connected to Professor Pargus in some tenuous way. It hurt to have such a suspicious mind-set but on occasion it's preferable to be safe than sorry.

'Wait!' he peered at Sam. 'I know you.'

'Do you?' said Sam.

'Yes! I've seen you here before. A few years back. You kept asking me if I had any carrots!'

'Oh…' said Sam.

'And did you?' I asked.

'No! Do I appear to be the kind of person who carries round carrots?'

'Frankly, yes.'

'Well, I did not! Had an apple on me, though. You said the other little bunnies would be delighted!'

'It was a crazy night,' said Sam.

'Did you thank me? No! You did not!'

'I thought I had hallucinated you.'

'Why would you think that?' The interrogator ran a hand through his moustache.

'Well, I'd like to thank you now. It was a great apple. Very tasty.'

'Better late than never! Pleased to meet you once again. Name's McCulloch!'

'I'm Sam, this is Cudgel.'

I stepped forward and shook McCulloch's hand. 'You don't happen to have any apples on you just now?' I asked.

'Not currently!' McCulloch looked around him. 'These are some dark woods. What brings you back here?'

Confident as I am about many things, seldom have I known the complete certainty I felt at this time. I needed to lie to McCulloch. I needed to lie to him so he would not have any suspicion whatsoever that Sam and I were looking for Professor Pargus's hideaway. Tell him that and the game would be given away for good. Tell him that and we were in real trouble.

What lie, though? I have a hard time lying. It's unedifying and I always have to fight the urge to laugh at the idea of people believing me. I needed a lie that was absolute and inarguable. A lie so potent that simply saying it would render any follow up questions obsolete. I took a deep breath. 'My uncle was killed by a deer. We're here for retribution, haha.'

'We're looking for Professor Pargus's hideaway,' said Sam

I had an unexpected moment of clarity. For a brief glimmer I understood why people hit me so much. It wasn't that they were angry with me, more that they were so shocked and confused that their only recourse was violence. But, of course, I would never hit Sam. Thus, lacking an outlet for my feelings, I found myself balling my hands then smacking them together several times while making an odd barking noise. I did not understand why she had said that.

'What!' said McCulloch.

'Uncle! Deer! Vengeance! Haha!' I said desperately.

172

'We're looking for Professor Pargus's hideaway. Would you be able to help us out?' said Sam, calmly.

'Kill the deer!' I tried to re-establish control of the narrative.

McCulloch punched me on the top of the head. I fell to the ground, getting my suit muddy beyond repair.

'Absolutely!' he said to Sam. 'Follow me!'

Flashlight in hand, he strode away, Sam and I scurrying to keep up. Abruptly, he turned left into the trees. I grabbed Sam.

'He's going into the trees,' I pointed out.

'Yes, we need to hurry or we'll lose him.'

'Why do we trust him? He didn't take my deer lie seriously at all.'

'Your lie was ridiculous.'

'Why was he so keen to help us find the Professor?'

McCulloch's flashlight was getting further away.

'Okay fine,' said Sam. 'I remembered that when I thought I was a rabbit, he had mentioned something about hating the Professor. Said he was a blight on the landscape.'

'Are you sure we can trust him?'

'It's either that or spend the night here.'

I thought of all the deer I may have angered with my lie and shuddered. 'Fine, let's follow him.'

The trees grew denser, blocking out the sky completely. With only McCulloch's flashlight to guide us, we descended further and further into the unknown. The silence taunted me. The longer we went the more the sense grew we were far beyond the reach of humanity.

'If McCulloch's secretly on the Professor's side we're in real trouble, eh?' I noted to Sam.

'I guess so,' she replied, which wasn't the reassuring answer I was hoping for.

'A little bit off the Heritage Trail this!' McCulloch called back to us. 'Nearly there though! In fact…'

He stopped and shone a light at the tree beside him. 'No, not this one!' He went to the tree next to it, then the one after that, peering at them intently. 'Not this one either! Ah…aha!' With great effort, and just a hint of showmanship, McCulloch pulled at one of the tree's branches.

'Does Professor Pargus live in a tree?' I asked.

'Don't be an idiot,' said Sam.

Suddenly there was a rumbling. The line of trees in front of us started to shake.

'Oh my God, it's the deer coming for us!' I cried.

The trees shook further, and began to part in the middle like a set of curtains. Wider and wider they opened, revealing behind them a large square shaped building.

'Here we are!' said McCulloch.

'Here we are,' said Sam.

'Bloody hell,' I added. From what I had understood, being a published author didn't pay nearly as well as it used to. I was compelled to conclude that there had to be some serious money in the international criminal game.

'So! I've brought you both here! What now?'

'It might be an idea to keep our voices down,' said Sam.

'Hmm! I see what you mean!' said McCulloch. 'I guess I'll try and talk a little quieter then. Not easy for me, mind!'

'Because of your moustache?' I asked.

'Partially deaf in one ear! Is this better?' He lowered his voice to somewhere slightly above a stage whisper.

'Much better,' said Sam.

'Let's bring the conversation back to the moustache, though,' I said.

'Maybe later.' McCulloch looked at us both in askance. 'Are you here to do something about Pargus?'

'We're here to catch him,' said Sam.

McCulloch nodded. 'Twenty years, I've watched over this place. Oversaw its construction, kept it hidden from passers-by, taken numerous bribes, decimated local wildlife. Do you know how long I've wanted someone to take Pargus down?'

'Twenty years?' I said.

'Fifteen! The first five were pretty good fun, if I'm being honest. Who wouldn't want to be part of a major conspiracy?' He continued, voice getting louder, 'But after a while I got bored of cleaning up his mess! But what could I do? Nothing! He owned me. Owned me!'

'Shh!' said Sam.

McCulloch didn't hear her. 'Then Moira left me! Of course she didn't know anything about anything. "You're keeping secrets" she'd say. And what could I say to that? She was right!'

'Shhh!' said Sam, more vehemently.

'And that's what drove you to the moustache?'

'Stop talking about the moustache!' shouted McCulloch.

'Never!'

'*Someone's going to hear us*,' said Sam.

'I've got a lot to get off my chest!' roared McCulloch, 'It's good to talk about these things!'

'He's right you know,' I said. 'It's bad to bottle stuff up. Let it all out, my man.'

'Now is *not* the time-….'

'Aaaaaaah!' McCulloch let out a primal yell, a noise so loud it shook both his moustache and the leaves on the apparently fake trees.

There followed a moment of calm.

'Hmm.' I began to see Sam's point. Shouting loudly and encouraging McCulloch to do the same could be construed as being detrimental to our plan of remaining incognito.

Damn my insatiable moustache curiosity. Still, as we stood now in silence it appeared there was no harm done. Then, a huge row of lights on the front of the building came on, illuminating everything around us. Professors Pargus's voice boomed.

'No one move,' he said, 'I've got a big gun pointing at all of you. Approach slowly, with your hands behind your head. See you soon, idiots.'

'Hmm,' I said again.

*

'...And then they told me they were out to catch you! So I double-bluffed them!'

I've heard it said that you should judge a man not by his words but his deeds. Now, McCulloch had been a great help in getting to Professor Pargus's secret hideaway, I would never deny that. And yes, he had seemed vehement in his distaste for the Professor and had explicitly stated he wanted to help us catch him. But to me at least, he let himself down by punching me on the back of the head and enthusiastically helping the large fellow tie Sam and I to a chair. They were good chairs, though. Of the hardback variety but finely crafted and accessorised with a fulsome cushion on the seat. Really, if this was being held as prisoner it wasn't so bad. If I'd only had the means to scratch my nose I daresay I would have been quite comfortable.

In lieu of a full tour we had been taken straight to the basement. With just a few leaking pipes and a single light bulb it was certainly minimalist in décor. Not at all what I would have expected from the Professor, a man for whom an ascot was a way of life. Even now, casually leaning on a shotgun, he looked wonderful in plaid pyjamas and a natty leopard print dressing gown.

'So, what you're saying, McCulloch, is that after finding these two, you had the presence of mind to bring them here, giving away the exact location of my very secret hideaway?'

'Correct!' replied McCulloch.

The Professor tapped his fingers on the shotgun thoughtfully. 'You understand, this presents me with a problem. See, while this place looks impressive, there's actually not as much room as you'd think.'

The building had actually looked fairly sizable to me, but with the Professor, McCulloch, the large fellow, Kenneth, as well as Sam and I all crammed into the basement, it was hard to argue that it didn't feel a little crowded.

'Why don't you just shoot them both?' said Kenneth, 'And then I can get some bloody sleep. The *day* I've had…'

Honestly, I was beginning to grow a little cold on Kenneth. Obviously our years of friendship would forever bind us together and he would perennially be one of my favourite people in the world but his behaviour recently had not been great. Faking his death for Mystery Man only to reveal himself to be in league with Professor Pargus the whole time may have seemed a fun idea, but in reality a lot of feelings had been hurt. And now, here he was,

181

saying that Sam and I should be shot. No, I was fast coming to the conclusion that Kenneth may not have been the man I thought he was.

'You always say that,' said the large fellow. 'But who's the one who has to clean up, eh?'

'That's what *you're* here for,' said Kenneth. 'That's your job.'

'Pfft,' retorted the large fellow.

'How dare you!' said Kenneth. 'You "Pfft" at me?'

'And what if I do, eh?'

Kenneth and the large fellow continued to bicker. Professor Pargus watched them with a benign boredom. How many arguments like this had he witnessed over the years? How many double crossings and late night hostage taking situations had he been party to? He leaned on the gun and for a moment looked very old indeed. It hurt to see him like this. I felt a jabbing sensation in my wrists. Tilting backwards I saw that it was not a physical manifestation of my sadness regarding Professor Pargus and the passage of time, but Sam trying to cut me free with what appeared to be a small blade. That she had managed to secrete such an item on her person was impressive, managing to cut herself free without anyone noticing doubly so. And to then choose to try and free me? I was very touched.

'Thanks,' I said.

She gave me a look which told me to immediately be quiet.

'I think that's about enough.' Professor Pargus picked up his shotgun. 'Kenneth, Alan, you know we don't argue in front of guests. We'll leave the room and talk through our differences like adults.'

'Yes, Professor Pargus,' said Kenneth and the large fellow sulkily.

'McCulloch, watch over these two. We'll be back shortly.'

The three of them climbed up the stairs and left the room, shutting the door behind them. I felt the ropes around my wrist fall. I was free.

McCulloch ran a hand through his moustache.

'I think I fooled them!' he exclaimed.

'What?' said Sam.

'I think they bought it! Can't you see, I double crossed them!'

'By hitting me on the head and tying us up?' I said

'Exactly! They won't suspect a thing! I'm a genius!'

I considered the matter, and was genuinely erring on the side on agreeing with him when the door opened.

'Now really,' said Professor Pargus. 'There we are outside trying to politely settle an argument and all we can hear is you banging on about double crossing us.'

'You really should speak more quietly, you know,' I said to McCulloch.

'I know!' said McCulloch, 'This kind of thing happens all the time! It's my fatal flaw!'

Without even being told to, he sat down beside us. 'We gave it our best shot eh!' he said to Sam and I.

'That's not a very can-do attitude,' I replied.

'Cudgel,' said Professor Pargus.

This was the first time the Professor had ever said my name. Close as we were, I had only been around forty per cent sure he knew what it was. It was a big deal for me and I wasn't going to let circumstances get in the way of enjoying it. I forgot about McCulloch and his loud voice, about Kenneth and his immoral actions, about the large fellow and the fact we hadn't really bonded. I forgot about all I had been through the past few days, that I was currently being held hostage and that Sam, sitting right beside me, had endeavoured to help me so much. I forgot about everything except that the Professor had said my name. Yes, indeed it was exciting times for me.

'Professor Pargus,' I replied.

'Stand up, Cudgel, I can see your hands are untied.'

Without a second thought, I stood up. Dimly, beside me I heard Sam mutter, 'Oh, for God's *sake*.'

'Come closer, Cudgel,' said the Professor, reaching the bottom of the stairs and beckoning me with the shotgun.

'Be careful, Professor,' I heard Kenneth say. 'He's an *idiot*.'

I moved closer. The prints on the Professor's dressing gown were themselves tiny leopards, replete with their own print. The attention to detail in the garment was a marvel.

'Excellent dressing gown, Professor.'

'Thank you, Cudgel. I got it in Rome.'

'Rome in Italy?'

'Yes. Have you ever wanted to go to Italy?'

Italy. The word flowed effortlessly through my ears and moved sylph-like round my other senses. Italy in my nostrils and mouth, fine wines and tomato based foodstuffs. Its welcoming heat

on my skin. Closing my eyes, in front of me. There was a whole

world outside of Glasgow I had never known. *Italy*. And France

and Spain. Belarus, Latvia. Egypt and Bolivia. Others countries

too, I had to imagine.

'I've underestimated you, Cudgel,' said the Professor. 'For

a long time, you were just a ridiculous person following Sally,

Donald, Hamish and Kenneth. I asked, and they assured me you

were no one I should concern myself with. But you know what?

There's a reason why I'm a criminal genius and bestselling author

and they aren't. One doesn't get to be a multi-hyphenate without

knowing a thing or two. Wisdom is knowing when you're wrong.

You're loyal, Cudgel. And resourceful. What's more, you have a

frankly frightening violent streak. Violence is an underrated quality

in a person. Violence is truth. Violence is power. For people like

you and me, Cudgel, violence is who we are.' Professor Pargus extended his hand. 'What do you say, Cudgel? Would you like to work for me, officially be part of the crew?'

I gazed down at the proffered hand. Wrinkly, yes. Clearly that of an older person. Framed by a sliver of pyjama sleeve and, of course, the dressing gown. My eyes met those of one of the tiny leopards. So strong and powerful. I'd read that a leopard could kill and eat you before you'd even had time to marvel at its spots. Majestic, yes, but ultimately untrustworthy. Or maybe that was too harsh, for the leopard merely did what came naturally to it. If you were caught by one, that was your fault as a hapless human for getting too close. Professor Pargus wanted me to be part of the group. He'd said it with his mouth in front of several witnesses. What to do?

I had a great deal to unpack from the past few days. From finding Kenneth dead to finding that Kenneth wasn't the person I thought he was, a lot had taken place. What lessons were to be gleaned? Probably some things about trust. Me, Kenneth, Donald,

188

Sally and Hamish – we were the five amigos. It had been Professor Pargus who had been the outsider, close to us, but not one of the core members. *And yet,* if I'd learned anything at all in this fantastic adventure, it was that there was a good chance I liked the group more than they liked me. It hurt bitterly to think it, but at last I knew it to be true. Now here was Professor Pargus offering me an official welcome into his inner sanctum. With a handshake no less - the most unbreakable of bonds. He had even said we were alike. Professor Pargus's acceptance would oblige the others to follow suit. This was everything I had ever wanted. I stuck out my hand.

'No!' said Sam.

'*No!*' said Kenneth.

Professor Pargus grinned as my hand inched closer to his. Never had I thought I'd be in this position but I knew what had to be done. I balled my hand into a fist and with all my might I punched Professor Pargus. He staggered backwards and fell against the wall.

'You idiot!' he said, eyes ablaze. 'You punch me? Punch me! Oh, you'll pay for that.' He raised the shotgun. Then the lights in the room went out.

It was as though someone had made me close my eyes, tied a blindfold round my head then stuck a balaclava backwards over my face. Certainly it was unnerving, yet also strangely calming. We were all in this pitch black room together and would be forced to let bygones be bygones and bind together to find a light source.

It became clear almost immediately that the majority of the room saw things a little differently. McCulloch was the first to speak. 'The lights have gone out!'

'I don't like this,' said the large fellow.

'Don't worry…Alan,' I said, thinking now was as good a time as ever to test the waters on using his name. 'We should bind together as a team to form a solution to our problem.' I said, with some eloquence.

'Yeah, and how do you suggest we do that?' Even in the current situation I could tell Sam was rolling her eyes at me.

'Form sub-committees maybe?' I said.

'God, you are *such* an idiot,' said Kenneth.

'Hey, don't say that about him,' said Sam.

'He's a maniac,' said the large fellow. 'Nearly killed us both in the car earlier!'

'That's a highly subjective reading of events!' I said.

'You grabbed the bloody wheel!'

'Time was of the essence!'

'That's *exactly* the sort of idiotic thing you always do!' said Kenneth.

'Not any more idiotic than faking your own death for no reason!' said Sam.

'I *had* a reason!'

'Good luck re-integrating back into society!' Sam said.

191

'I think I've missed several key points of the day!' said McCulloch.

'Silence!' said Professor Pargus.

At once all was quiet. Enveloped in darkness and with the only sound in the room a dripping pipe, there was a tension in the air. My attempts at building a consensus had failed and it looked as though Professor Pargus was about to take the initiative. It was then that it really hit home; I had punched Professor Pargus. Punched his face. There was no getting past it and no denying it. A roomful of witnesses had seen me do it. My breathing quickened and I gulped like a guilty fish. My hero, my idol. The man who had written all of those wonderful books, finding poetry in potatoes and bravely seeking lyricism in the travails of intergalactic super-rodents. It was clear that my life was now delineated into two periods – pre and post punching Professor Pargus. And *yet*…and yet it had definitely seemed the right thing to do. And even as I stood in the darkness, I still felt that overall, I had made the right choice. Searching my brain, soul, and gut, I located a strange sensation permeating all three. It was an unfamiliar feeling, dusty and creaking from disuse. I couldn't quite believe it. Yes, my abiding feeling having punched Professor Pargus was pride. I was feeling very proud of myself.

'Feeling proud of yourself?' said Professor Pargus.

'Argh,' I said, then realised he didn't seem to be addressing me.

'Feeling good? Feel like you've bested me?'

'Um…Professor,' said Kenneth. 'Which of us are you *talking* to?'

'He knows,' said Professor Pargus. 'He knows I'm talking to him.'

An expectant silence followed these words. Time ticked on, still no one responding.

'It's not me you're talking to, is it?' bellowed McCulloch.

'I know you're here, Detective Arnold,' said Professor Pargus.

Mystery Man. Good God, could it be true? In all of the excitement, I had rather forgotten about him.

'Reveal yourself,' said Professor Pargus. 'I've got a shotgun. Reveal yourself or I'll start firing. I'm bound to hit you at some point.'

'That's not really good news for any of us!' remarked McCulloch.

If Mystery Man really was here he knew how to draw out anticipation. Even with the threat of being indiscriminately sprayed with shotgun bullets it was hard not to feel a sense of excitement, to really soak in the drama of the occasion. There was a high pitched shrieking immediately recognisable as Kenneth. An instant later the light turned on. Holding a gun to Kenneth's head, a manic glint in his eye, was Mystery Man.

'Yo!' I said. 'You managed to find us.'

'Hamish gave me incredibly detailed instructions. After that it was all about biding my time.' Mystery Man re-doubled his grip on Kenneth's neck.

'Um, *ouch*?' said Kenneth.

Professor Pargus stepped forward. With the lights back on, it was clear my punch had really hit home. His right eye had already swollen a significant degree. Now, there were clearly moral implications in regards to hitting an old man in the face, but I wasn't about to set foot in that grey area. I saw only a perfect shot, which, on balance, had been absolutely merited.

'Good of you to make it, Detective,' said Professor Pargus.

'It's over, Pargus,' said Mystery Man. 'Give up or I swear I'll shoot him.'

'Now, *hang* on...' interjected Kenneth.

'Come on now, Mystery Man,' I said. 'You're a peaceful fellow. You don't really want to shoot anyone. Even if they are a duplicitous lowlife like Kenneth.' I surprised myself with my candour.

'You don't know what I'll do!' shouted Mystery Man. I saw in his eyes a deep rage. This was a man obsessed with catching Professor Pargus. He would stop at no lengths to do so. Given the last few days, I maybe should have cottoned onto this a little quicker.

'So, what'll it be, Pargus? Eh!' said Mystery Man.

Professor Pargus gave the matter several seconds thought. 'Fair enough, go ahead and shoot him.'

'*What*?' said Kenneth.

'You've outlived your usefulness to me, I think even you'd agree with that.'

'I faked my bloody death for you. Even my *wife* thinks I'm dead.'

Professor Pargus smiled and spoke slowly and patiently. 'And as such, you're incredibly expendable.'

'Can't argue with that logic,' chimed the large fellow.

Kenneth was not happy. 'I-..but-…This is all incredibly *unfair.*'

'Such is life,' shrugged the Professor.

'Is this because of *Journey of the Space Ferret*? That's why you're letting me die?'

'In some ways, no. But in real terms, yes, it's had a significant impact on my thinking.'

'Enough!' said Mystery Man. He pushed the gun harder against Kenneth's head. 'I decide who lives and dies. I'm giving you one last chance, Pargus. Surrender or I'll shoot.'

'Well, I think I've just made my position abundantly clear.'

It appeared the die had well and truly been cast. All we could do as a group was watch. Mystery Man put his finger on the trigger. Kenneth closed his eyes. Professor Pargus looked on with mild interest. The large fellow stood slack-jawed and McCulloch

197

ran a pensive hand through his moustache. Beside me, Sam grabbed my hand and I hers. It was a heavy moment.

Without warning, Mystery Man quickly raised his gun towards the ceiling and fired at the light bulb, casting us once again into darkness, smashed pieces of glass in our hair.

'Am I dead? Is this heaven?' said Kenneth.

'Attack!' cried Professor Pargus, and fired his shotgun. I was pretty sure he hadn't caught anyone, but it seemed he had hit one of the pipes as water started spraying round the room. The darkness awoke something animalistic in all of us. People were shouting, but it wasn't in any language I understood. We had regressed into an ancient form of humanity, beyond the scope of mere words. Because, truly, there were no more words to be said, no cases to argue. All that was left was combat, the oldest of human rituals. It was my time to shine.

'Ouch!' I yelped. I had felt a small hand grab my leg then pinch me.

'Sorry, didn't realise it was you,' said Sam. 'Got a little carried away.'

'I understand,' I said, ripping off my shirt and tying it round my head.

I charged forward and began throwing punches. Sam was behind me, so I knew I wouldn't hit her. Accidentally catching Mystery Man was a worry but I felt overall he would accept being punched as the price one must pay in this sort of scenario. Alas, my path forward was abruptly halted by a long metallic object sticking in my gut.

'Oooft,' I said.

'I've got you, Cudgel,' whispered Professor Pargus in my ear. 'This is what happens when you punch me. I'm going to shoot you now.' He jabbed the gun into me again.

'Oooft. Arguably the two actions don't entirely equate.'

This was it then. This was the end. I suppose there were worse ways to go than to be shot by one's former hero in the

199

middle of a mass brawl in the dark in his basement. More prosaic ways, at least. Still, there had been so much more I had wanted to do. The last few days had shown me a world I hadn't known existed. I was keen to explore it, exchange pleasantries with it, feel its contours. But it seemed it was not to be. I sighed, closed my eyes and hoped against hope I had tensed my stomach muscles enough.

'Ow!' cried Professor Pargus, falling to the floor.

'*Got* you!'

'You hit *me*, you fool,' said Professor Pargus.

'Oh,' said Kenneth. '*Ah.*'

'Now I can't find my shotgun. And I was just about to shoot Cudgel. Honestly, Kenneth, you are useless.'

'It was an *accident*.'

'That's all fine and well, but now I'm down a shotgun.'

The Professor scrabbled on the ground, searching. Beneath my feet I felt the shotgun. With my right foot I stamped hard on the

Professor's hand, simultaneously using the left to flick the gun backwards.

'Ow!' said Professor Pargus. 'My bloody hand.'

I stood for a moment, proud of my handiwork. As it transpires, this is decidedly not the thing to do in the middle of a multi-person fight in the dark. Two figures, who I presumed were Mystery Man and the large fellow embroiled in battle, crashed into me, sending me to the ground.

'I've got the shotgun,' whispered Sam to me, patting my head.

'Alright, enough!' shouted Professor Pargus. 'Alan, let's get out of here.'

The large fellow grunted in affirmative, and following what sounded like some heavy duty scraping and flailing, Mystery Man was thrown into the corner beside Sam and me.

'Cudgel, if they escape…I blame you,' said Mystery Man. The fight with the large fellow had clearly sent him out of his right mind, which was confirmed by him passing out on my shoulder.

There was the sound of stairs being clambered, and then the door to the basement opening. Light from upstairs swung around the room, catching each of us in the face. Professor Pargus and the large fellow were gone.

'Oh, don't wait for *me*, then,' said Kenneth. He glanced over to Sam and I. 'Honestly, the *Professor* sometimes…' Quickly, he realised that whatever the merits of his gripes with the Professor, we were decidedly the wrong crowd to be relaying them to.

'I'll be off then,' he said and headed towards the stairs. He managed to plant his one foot on the bottom step before Sam leapt at him and grabbed his other leg.

'Not so fast,' she said.

'Get *off.*'

'Absolutely not.'

'Why *not*?'

'Don't want you to escape. Is that not obvious?'

With an angry sigh, Kenneth lifted his other leg and kicked Sam hard on the shoulder. She let out a sharp cry of pain and fell to the ground. Kenneth ran up the stairs and out of the basement.

I hurried over to Sam. 'How is your shoulder? I saw Kenneth kick you there.'

Her skin was even paler than usual. 'It's fine. Go and catch them.'

I was loathe to leave both an injured Sam and an unconscious Mystery Man in the basement. On the other hand, I was feeling a rage like I had never known. I wanted to catch the three of them and inflict some injury. Well, perhaps mostly to Kenneth and the Professor. There was still an outside chance the large fellow and I could be friends. I started up the stairs.

'Wait!' said a voice from the other side of the room. It was McCulloch, who, to be honest, I had totally forgotten about.

203

'Take this!' He handed me his torch. 'Maybe I should have used it when it was all dark there and everyone was fighting! Ah well! Good luck, Cudgel!'

I looked down at Sam.

'Good luck, Cudgel,' she said. 'Will you take the shotgun?'

'No need,' I pointed to the torch. 'I have this.'

Mystery Man said nothing, as he was still unconscious.

*

It was cold outside and I replaced my shirt from around my head to its rightful position. Though the large lights were still illuminating the open ground all around me, it was going to be tricky to find anyone once I got to the trees.

'Wait for *me*!' I heard a distant voice whine. It was too far away to be absolutely certain it was Kenneth calling out to the Professor and the large fellow. For all I knew, there could be dozens of other people having dozens of other exciting adventures in the trees. Nonetheless, in pressurised situations one is always best going with their gut. And though mine was still a little tender from having a shotgun shoved in it, it was telling me to follow that voice.

In school I had never been the greatest of runners. My style was far too idiosyncratic to fit in the neatly defined parameters of a 'traditional' running track. Eventually, my habit of encroaching on others' space before shoving them out of the way had led to me being banned from competing. Embittered, I had vowed to prove myself to be one of the greatest runners the country had ever known. Admittedly, this was something I had still to get round to, but chasing after Kenneth right now seemed as good a place as any to start the process. My legs moving furiously, I was swiftly in the trees.

'*Don't* leave without me!' cried the voice, nearer now. I was definitely making progress. I continued to run, affecting a remarkable array of swerves and pirouettes to avoid hitting any of the trees. Above me, the sky was a purple bruise; it was nearly

dawn. The trees were thinning now, the path in front of me lighter.

In the distance I could see Kenneth running ahead of me.

'Aha!' I cried. 'There you are, Kenneth! I see you running

in front of me. I'm going to catch you!' Kenneth glanced

backwards and I saw the fear and surprise in his eyes. Suddenly he

disappeared. One moment he was in front of me then he was gone.

Continuing to run, I came to a steep hill. I looked down and saw

that it led to the loch. Kenneth was scrambling towards the water,

where Professor Pargus and the large fellow were sitting in a

speedboat. Again, I took a second to appreciate the serious wealth

Professor Pargus had accumulated over the course of his varied

careers. I mean, a getaway speedboat? That was money right there.

'Here I am,' said Kenneth, getting to the bottom of the hill

and moving slowly towards the boat. He was wheezing heavily and

appeared very much out of breath. Really, he wasn't in good shape at all. Maybe faking one's death has a greater effect than one might think.

'Not so fast!' I said. The hill was rather steep and getting down safely would take more time and effort than I had. There was only one thing for it. Arching my arm back, with all my might I hurled McCulloch's torch at Kenneth, aiming for the sweet spot where lower back met upper leg. It landed some twelve feet from its intended target. Improvising furiously, I lay sideways on the ground and, in time honoured egg-rolling fashion, tilted myself sideways and down the hill.

Gaining pace with every roll until I surrendered control of the project to gravity, all I can recall thinking was that perhaps I should have at least given some consideration to just trying to run down the hill. Kenneth was hunched over, dry retching. Seriously, he needed to join a gym or something. My momentum carried me nearer and nearer until finally I rolled into him like a bowling ball hitting a skittle.

'Strike!' I cried, which may have been the funniest thing anyone has ever said. Kenneth didn't see it that way. He groggily got to his feet and pulled a gun out of his pocket.

'Damn it, Cudgel, I'm going to enjoy this.'

Despite being incredibly dizzy, I jumped at him. The gun flew from his hand and landed beside us. I was happy to leave it there, but Kenneth had other ideas so again we were forced to wrestle for it.

'We're leaving now,' said Professor Pargus in a bored voice.

'Wait!' said Kenneth, scrambling to his feet towards them. He shoved me aside and started to run very slowly towards the boat.

'Stop them!' shouted a voice behind me. I turned to see Mystery Man and Sam at the top of the hill. The large fellow revved the engine. Kenneth was close to them. With a final effort I rushed forward and executed a textbook slide tackle. The engine grew louder. Professor Pargus stood and gazed up to the top of the hill.

'Better luck next time, Arnold!' He looked back towards Kenneth and I. 'Well played, Cudgel,' he said, saluting me. 'I'm sure we'll meet again.'

The boat began to move. Mystery Man and Sam joined us at the bottom of the hill.

'He got away,' said Mystery Man disconsolately.

'For now,' said Sam. 'He'll be back.'

'All of it. All of that time and effort for nothing.'

I put one arm around Mystery Man and the other round Sam, pinning Kenneth to the ground with my heel. Together we looked out onto the loch, where the sun was beginning to rise and the only speck on the horizon was the speedboat moving ever further from us. Even over the noise of the engine, the faint sound of Professor Pargus cackling could still be heard.

`   'Not for nothing,' I said. 'We had an adventure, did we

not?'

25164816R00125

Printed in Great Britain
by Amazon